Unveiled

SECRETS OF THE DAGGER

Book 3

SASHA R.C.

NEWMAN SPRINGS PUBLISHING
320 Broad Street
Red Bank, NJ 07701

First originally published by Newman Springs Publishing 2022

ISBN 979-8-88763-100-4 (Paperback)
ISBN 979-8-88763-101-1 (Digital)

Printed in the United States of America

Acknowledgments

J eff Christophersen for being my biggest fan and my manager.

Leroy and Janis Christophersen for believing in me and supporting my dreams of wanting to be an author.

Karen Prosser for being my best friend and my cheerleader.

To all my readers, I appreciate all of you and you being willing to go on this journey with me. The story of Sky is just beginning. I hope you all enjoy the twists and turns and secrets that finally come to the surface.

Introduction

We were able to make it through the levels of hell; not many people have been able to make it out not changed. The thing is, Damon, Daniel, and I are changed; we just don't know exactly what we have all changed into.

My bond with my mates survived; we were able to work together for the most part and make it through and save Daniel. He has changed. Daniel's and Damon's marks have switched—Damon now white, Daniel now black. We have no idea what it means, but it must have something to do with them now having wings.

Now we are waiting, watching, preparing for what is to come. Barbas is sure to come out of his hellhole soon enough and claim me as his own. He is determined to make me his and have me by his side.

The only hope we have at stopping him is finding the broken pieces of the dagger and going to the waters of Edanya and putting it back together again. Michael, one of the remaining pure-breed Angels, is planning on helping us, for he is the only one that knows of Edanya's location.

Michael says he is here to protect me, to watch over me, but I have a feeling that he is searching for answers to something that will end up changing everything again.

Prologue

Light blade, a.k.a. the Dagger.

It has been set forth that a blade created from heaven, hell, and earth will be forged.

The dagger will wield great power.

The dagger is not of the light or the dark.

The dagger will wield the ability to take any being's powers.

The dagger is the key to ending the war.

The dagger has many secrets.

The dagger will not take sides, for it does not have allegiance to either side.

Only an Angel, a pure breed, may speak of the hidden magic within.

CHAPTER 1

Where to Begin?

Three months later

It has been three months since Michael blue beamed us out of hell, three months since we finally got Daniel back; nothing is the way it was. I sit back and watch my mates; they stay as far away from each other as they can, only coming together when I ask them to.

The soul-bond with my mates is getting stronger; our connection is getting deeper. I try to spend time with both of them on their own, making sure that they both know that I love them. Daniel is still guarded, and he will not speak about everything they did to him while he was in hell.

Honestly we are still trying to recover from what the levels brought out in each of us. Michael also keeps his distance and stays away when my mates are around me. He is different when it is just him and me together. I see something in him that hasn't been there before—compassion, longing, desire.

The cottage has become all of our home. We each do chores and have made it our own. I think Daniel is waiting for me to be fully ready to connect to him like I have with Damon, but to tell you the truth, I don't think I am ready just yet.

The idea of being fully connected to both of them in every way possible still sends my head spinning in a million directions. Michael has told me that it is normal to be connected to both of them, but inside my mind, I feel that I am harming one when I am with the other; this mate thing is way more complicated than I ever thought was possible.

I stare up at the ceiling in my room, trying to find the energy and motivation to get up. I need to talk to Daniel, Damon, and Michael and figure out what we need to do. Just sitting around here, acting as if everything is normal is driving me insane.

I take a deep breath and throw my covers off of me. I swing my legs over to the side of the bed and push myself up. My body feels heavy; I don't know the last time I actually got some sleep, like actually sleep. I sit there for a moment. I can hear the men in the living room talking, patiently waiting for me to get up.

I gently put my feet on the cold floor and make my way over to my mirror across the room. The reflection staring back at me in this moment is someone I don't recognize; I have bags under my eyes, my skin is paler than normal, my stomach makes a loud hungry noise. I place my hands on my stomach and grab the sweater that is on the back of the chair.

I pull it over my head and walk over to the door. I put my hand on the doorknob and take another deep breath; we have all learned how to take deep breaths. I turn the doorknob and push the door open and take a step into the narrow hallway. As soon as I do, I can feel the warmth from the fireplace hit my face.

I close the door and slowly make my way down the hallway toward the living room. All the men stop talking when I come out from the hallway and start making my way toward the couch. Damon is sitting in the chair, Daniel is sitting the couch, and Michael is leaning against the brick wall by the fireplace; all of their eyes are on me. I make my way to the couch and take a seat next to Daniel. I watch him take his hand and put it on my leg.

"What are you guys talking about?" I ask, looking from Daniel to Damon, then to Michael. None of them say anything at first; they all just stare at me.

Finally Damon clears his throat. "We were talking about what we need to do."

"And?" I reply to him.

"And what our plan should be," Damon states, clearing his throat again.

Since being back at the cottage, all of the men have been acting very odd; they all appear to not know how to act around one another, or me when we are all together, which is strange because Damon and Michael are very confident, and Daniel found his voice when we were going through the levels of hell together.

"What is our plan?" I state, looking over to Michael, his eyes locking onto mine.

"We need to find the dagger, for starters…," Michael states.

"Well, that is going to be harder than what you think," Daniel states.

I look from Michael to Daniel.

"Why is that?"

"Because when I was being tortured and held in that room, I was able to overhear many things, and one of them is that Barbas had Argo break the dagger into three different pieces, and then he went out and hid them. He is the only one that knows where they are," Daniel states, looking from me to Michael.

"Well, then that does make things more complicated," Michael states.

"You think?" I state, trying to hide my annoyed tone.

"Sky, we will find a way," Daniel states, squeezing my leg.

"How? How in the world are we going to find a way? Argo is in hell, remember?" I state, looking over to Damon; his eyes are dead set on mine. I watch him take a deep breath and release it as slow as he can.

"Don't worry, Sky…none of are going back into hell," Michael states.

"Really?" I state, not hiding my irritation from any of them.

I turn and look at Michael; he nods. "Yes, really," he states in a calm voice. I have always been amazed with how Michael can be the calm in the storm. I have only seen him lose his temper a few times, and they have been mainly pointed toward me and my actions.

"Then how the hell are we going to learn where the pieces are?" I state.

"We are going to let him come to us," Damon states.

"What in the world makes you all think that he will come to us?" I ask, even more confused.

I look at each of my mates, and then to Michael, all of them are staring at me. I shake my head. "Me? I'm the bait, is that right?" Michael nods.

"Of course... I should have known," I state as I roll my eyes.

"We won't let nothing happen to you, Sky," Michael states.

"Sky, it is the only way to get him to come here," Daniel states, squeezing my leg.

"That is easy for all of you to say. You are not the one being hung out like a piece of meat," I state, pushing myself up and off of the couch.

Daniel stands up after me; he grabs my arm. "Sky, you are not a piece of meat," he states in a gentle voice.

I turn and look at Daniel; his eyes are searching mine, trying to comfort me, but in this moment, I just want to be alone. I don't want anyone trying to calm my emotions or trying and changing them. I take a deep breath and slowly make my way to the back door. I turn slightly around to look at the men; they are all staring at me.

I turn back around and put my hand on the doorknob. I start to turn it and see Damon state in my mind that he loves me, and nothing bad is going to happen. I tell him that I love him, too, and I turn the doorknob, push the door open, and walk outside. The door closes behind me. I make my way to the wooden bench down by the small wooden shed.

The sky is cloudy; it feels like it will rain soon.

I take a seat and try to calm my nerves.

CHAPTER 2

Nothing Is What It Appears to Be

Michael

I walk Sky walk out of the back door. I turn and look at Daniel and Damon; Damon is still sitting in the chair, and Daniel is standing, still watching Sky walk down to the wooden bench.

"I knew she would not take the plan well," Damon states, sitting back in the chair.

"Maybe we should think of something else...like, Michael, you blue beaming Argo back here," Daniel states, slowly lowering himself back down on the couch.

I shake my head. "That would not work," I state.

"Why?" Daniel asks while sitting back in the couch.

"Because remember, demons can't blue beam," I state.

Daniel shakes his head. "Well, then what else can we come up with?"

"Nothing...let me go talk to her...she will be fine" I state pushing myself off of the stone...

"You? You want to go talk to her?" Daniel asks.

I nod. "Yes, Daniel, I want to go talk to her...," I state as I turn around and head toward the back door.

"What will you say to her?" I hear Damon ask as I put my hand on the doorknob.

I don't turn around but just simply state, "The truth."

5

"And what trust is that?" Damon asks, not hiding his irritation.

"You will all know in due time," I state as I turn the doorknob and open the door.

I walk outside, and the door closes behind me, leaving Daniel and Damon in there alone to think about what I just stated. There is no time to argue about all of this; the more time we waste talking, the more dangerous Barbas and all of this becomes. The sooner we can start looking for the dagger, the better.

I stand there for a moment, looking down at Sky. She is staring at the small wooden shed. I can hear her breathing; it is heavy.

I make my way down to her. The wind is starting to pick up a little bit; the clouds are rolling in. I can smell that it is going to rain soon.

I get down to her and make my way in front of her. She continues to look at the shed.

I bend down on one knee in front of her, blocking her line of sight to the shed. I watch her take a deep breath and connect her eyes to mine.

"I have to be the bait, don't I?" Sky states.

I nod. "Yes...but nothing will happen to you, Sky... I give you my word," I state in a calm voice.

"Your word?" she states.

I nod again. "Yes."

"What is your word worth exactly?" she states in a stern voice.

"What do you mean, Sky?" I ask, trying to hide my confusion.

"You are telling me to trust you...you are telling me that you are here to watch over me...to protect me...and now you are telling me that you give me your word that nothing will happen. But how can I fully take you at your word after everything that has happened? Michael, I trust you... I do...but I am still on the fence of why you are here and what the hell is exactly going on," Sky states, standing up from the bench. She stands there, looking at me, waiting for me to respond.

"Sky, I am sorry for what I have done. I was wrong, but I promise you that my intentions are pure," I state, searching her eyes, her face. I watch her process my words.

She nods and starts walking toward the fence; I follow. She leans against the fence with her shoulder, continuing to watch me.

"Sky," I whisper.

"Michael," she whispers back.

"I really am sorry for taking your wings…and for asking you to choose. I have been doing a lot of research of the soul-bond and the prophecy of the chosen women…and I think I finally am able to understand why what I was asking you was impossible," I state.

She continues to look at me with eager eyes, wanting me to go on and say more.

"There are a lot of myths and legends out there, Sky. I haven't been able to figure out the correct one yet, but I promise once I do, you will be the first one that I tell," I state, watching her.

"Okay… I will be the bait," she states.

"You will?" I ask, surprised.

"Yes…but only if you do something for me," she states, looking deeper into my eyes.

"What?" I state, trying to prepare for what she is about to ask of me.

"Don't lie to me…okay?" she states in a calm voice.

I nod. "I won't lie."

She nods and pushes herself off of the fence and starts heading over to the hidden door.

I turn around to watch her. "Where are you going?" I ask in a concerned voice.

"To get more air… I won't be long," she states, continuing to make her way toward the wooden door, leading to the outside world.

"Sky, I don't think that is a good idea. At least let me go with you," I state, taking a step toward her.

"I will be fine, just wait here," she states as she gets to the door and puts her hand on the doorknob. "If you anything goes wrong, you will be able to hear me," she states as she opens the door and takes a step into the open field. I don't have time to respond before she closes the door behind her.

CHAPTER 3

Watch but Don't Be Seen

Argo

Since the Angel Michael came to hell and helped Sky, Daniel, and Damon escape, hell has been scrambling; all the demons are trying to buff up the security so next time we will be alerted before the Angel can get all the way through hell. An Angel has never attempted to go into hell and has never been able to help someone escape from it. The demons are in an uproar, wanting to speak to the prince, but so far he has not allowed anyone to enter his quarters but me.

My men are going insane trying to figure out what we should do. We have continued to kidnap fallens and have been successful in changing them into demons. Since Sky has escaped hell and has not returned for them, they have given into the darkness a lot faster than ever before. The screams fill the hallways as each fallen member gives into the evil we have exposed them to.

I make my way up the cold stone stairs up to the living quarters. The hallway is bare, cold; the demons are all in the lower level, trying to prepare the new army for what is coming. I need to talk to the prince and figure out our next course of action. We have been sitting in hell for months, just waiting for him to come out.

I slowly make my way down the hallway and stop when I get to his door. I walk up to the door and put my hand on the doorknob and gently knock with my other hand. I wait; at first there is no noise at all, no voice telling me to come in. I knock again and hear the prince tell me to enter.

I turn the doorknob and push the door open. There are still bottles on the floor, all empty and old; the room smells like a stale bar. I take a step inside and look over to the fireplace. The prince is sitting in his chair with a bottle in one hand and a glass in another; he has been drinking again, unable to stay sober since his encounter in the woods with Sky and Michael.

I take another few steps into the room; the door closes behind me. I stand there watching the prince, waiting for him to turn and look at me, but he doesn't; he just takes another gulp out of the glass.

After a few minutes, I finally give in and make my way to the prince. I walk over to the fireplace and lean my shoulder against the wall, watching the prince take one more gulp from his glass. He immediately refills the glass.

"My prince...you have to come out of your room," I state, watching his every move.

He takes another gulp. "I don't have to do anything, Argo." His head slowly turns toward me, his eyes lock with mine.

"The men—" I begin to state, but he cuts me off before I can say another word.

"The men can wait for my orders...just as you do," he states.

I nod.

"I want you to go to her, Argo."

I stand there, just staring at him. He has to be joking. It has to just be the whiskey talking, right?

"Did you hear me, Argo?" the prince states, taking another gulp out of the glass. I watch him refill it again.

"My prince...you want me to go to Sky?" I ask, trying to hide any sign of disapproval from him.

I watch him nod. "Yes...go to her...to them...but stay in the shadows," he states, looking from me to the fire.

I take a deep breath and slowly make my way around the prince and get to the marble table and grab the new bottle of whiskey on the table. I rip off the top and take a big gulp. I walk back over to where

I was before, with the bottle in my hand. The prince looks from the fire to the bottle in my hand and slowly looks up into my eyes.

"Make sure that you report back to me every few days. I want to know everything, every little detail about her...about all of them," he states, continuing to look into my eyes.

"What am I looking for, my prince?" I state.

"Their weaknesses. I need to know their blind spots so I can get to her again," he states as he looks back at the fire.

"And what about the men?" I state, taking another gulp from the bottle.

"What about the men?" the prince states, not hiding his anger.

"My prince, you need to go out to them and talk to them. They are getting restless. You need to calm them down before they lose their minds," I state in a concerned tone.

"There you go again, trying to tell me what I need to do. The men will be fine, just tell them to stay put until I tell them otherwise. You think you can do that, Argo?" the prince states, turning his head and looking at me again.

I nod.

"Good...now go. We have wasted enough time. The more we know about them—about her—and what they are planning, the sooner we can attack," he states, trying to keep his emotions under control.

"Yes, my prince," I state. I turn and start walking toward the door.

I am only inches away from the door when I hear the prince whisper, "And, Argo?"

"Yes, my prince," I state, not turning around to face him.

"Don't fail me...because if you do...it will be the last time," he states.

"Yes, my prince." I put my hand on the doorknob and turn it. The door swings open. I take a few steps into the hallway and turn around to face the prince one last time. He is looking into the fire, dazed, lifting the bottle to his mouth when the door closes shut.

I stand there for a moment, the bottle still in my hand. I take a deep breath. I need to trust him. I need to try and trust him. He knows what he is doing.

I start walking down the hallway to the secret staircase that leads to the surface. Barbas wanted it to be created so we could get in and out of hell without going through the levels.

I make my way down the hallway to the staircase. It is narrow, dark; it is a long way up to the top. I am thankful, for it will give me time to think about what I need to do.

I start making my way up the staircase, getting lost in my own thoughts. Since Barbas has taken over as the prince of darkness, everything we have been doing lately only has to do with his plan to get Sky; everything else has been neglected, forgotten about.

There is nothing I can do but follow the orders and do what is asked of me to do. I only wish the men could do the same. I have noticed, and Barbas will soon, how the men have been thinking more and more on their own. This is a dangerous game, and if it is not played well, we will all lose at the end.

One hour later

I have been making my way up the staircase for a while now. I look up toward the sky and finally see the light at the top. Each step I take gets me closer and closer to following through with my orders.

I take a deep breath and continue walking up the last fifteen steps. I make my way up the last step and enter the surface. The breeze is cold; the sky is filled with clouds getting ready to release their rain. I look around and see the jungle. It is still; it is quiet. A storm is coming, and the jungle and the animals are preparing for it to come.

I close my eyes and enter into the shadows. It is time to follow through with my orders.

CHAPTER 4

What Don't I Know?

I close the wooden door behind me and make my way to the field. I can tell that Michael is not agreeing with my choice to leave and go out in the open, but I just need time to think. Everything is happening so fast.

As I make my way through the field and toward the forest, the clouds release the drops that have been waiting to be set free. The smell of the fresh fallen raindrops fill my nose and bring me a comfort I haven't felt in a long time.

I look forward and see the forest. The last time I set foot into this forest, Barbas found me. I am hoping this time, he doesn't get in the same results as before. I just want to be left alone so I can think about everything that has happened and will be happening in the near future.

The reasons I started this journey at the beginning no longer exists; everything has changed. Honestly I am losing sight in what we are trying to achieve. Before, I was dead set on killing the prince of darkness; now I am just trying to make it to where we all survive just one more day.

The moment I think things are going to be easier, there are more twists and turns that I never saw coming; more pieces to the puzzle are being revealed. I continue to make my way through the field and stop when I am only a few feet away from entering into the forest. I can hear Daniel and Damon in my head, both of them asking me to please be careful. I know if it was up to them, they would both come with me.

Everyone wants to be with me all the time. I just need some space. I feel as if I am losing air; I need space to breath and process my own thoughts instead of my mates' thoughts. I have allowed their thoughts to take over; they are becoming more dominant than my own. I take a breath and take the last few steps to enter into the threshold of the forest. The rain is falling through the trees; the ground is wet, muddy. I slowly make my way down the same path I walked before.

The trees are quiet, welcoming the rain into their roots; the roots of this forest are strong. Mother Earth is still hanging on, keeping what power she has left. I make my way down the pathway. I come up on the spot that Barbas came out of the shadows and attacked me. I slightly turn around and look around, trying to make sure that I am alone. I release a breath and shake my head.

All of this is finally getting to my head. I turn back around and see a man standing in front of me. I slowly take a step back, and when I do, he takes a step forward out of the trees. I stop and see that it is Gabriel. He stands still. He is tall, strong; his eyes are soft but stern. He takes another step forward.

"Sky, you have nothing to fear from me. You should know that," Gabriel states, taking another step forward.

"I do not fear you, Gabriel. I am surprised, that is all," I state, looking around to see if he is alone.

"I am alone, Sky. Like I stated, you have nothing to fear from me," Gabriel states, taking another step forward.

"Why are you here?" I state, watching him.

"I came to talk to you, Sky. There are things you need to know," Gabriel states, getting even closer to me.

"What don't I know?" I ask in a whisper.

"Young Sky, there is plenty that you don't know," Gabriel says in a whisper.

I stand there, waiting for him to say more, but he doesn't; he just looks at me. I go to turn around, and I feel him close the remaining distance between us, and grab my arm. I look down at his hand and then look up to his face.

"Sky, please don't go," Gabriel states, his eyes searching mine.

"I don't have time for your games, Gabriel. I came out here to think, not to try to understand your riddles," I state.

I watch him shake his head. "I am not trying to play games with you," he states in a stern voice.

"It feels like games, and I have played enough games lately," I state calmly, taking my arm out of his hand.

I watch him back away and run his hands through his hair. "I can't tell you everything, Sky. There are some things that you are not ready to know."

"Then tell me what I am ready to know," I state, backing away from him even more.

He watches me back away. He closes his eyes and shakes his head. "The prophecy that you have heard so much about…it is about you, Sky."

He opens his eyes and looks at me. "How do you know that?" I state.

"Because of your marks…because of you having more than one mate…because of how you all have changed since surviving the levels of hell…"

"Gabriel, it is just a piece of paper that was created centuries ago. We don't even know what it means…," I state in a stern voice.

"I know what it means, and I know what you are…what you all are," Gabriel states, taking a small step toward me.

I want to turn and walk away, but I can't. If he really does know what we are and what the prophecy means, I need to hear it. I am sick and tired of everyone keeping secrets.

I throw my hands in the air and yell, "Well, if you know, then tell me!"

"Like I said, you are not ready to know everything," he states.

I decide to be bold and quickly close the distance between us. I am now only inches away from him, close enough to feel the heat off of his body, close enough to feel his breath come across my face.

"What am I?" I state.

I watch Gabriel take a deep breath. "Sky."

"Gabriel…just tell me!" I yell.

"You are all protectors!" he yells back.

I take a small step back.

"Protectors? What the hell are protectors? I have never heard of them," I state.

"Sky, protectors are a breed of warriors that were created to keep the balance between light and dark. The protectors' job is to simply protect," he states, keeping his eyes locked with mine.

"So like fallens and Angels?"

I watch him shake his head. "No, Sky. Protectors are nothing like the fallen or like the Angels. Protectors have special abilities that neither fallen nor Angels have."

I take another step back. "I am a half-breed, remember?"

I watch him shake his head again. "Not anymore. You are not fallen or human…you are indeed a protector."

"How do you know?" I ask, trying to keep my emotions in check.

"Because of your wings…because of your mates…because I am one of the only Angels left that can sense your power," Gabriel states, watching me closely.

"This makes no sense at all—none. Daniel is human, and Damon—well, he is now a demon!" I yell.

"No, Sky, they used to be a human and a demon. You have seen their wings. They are protectors just like you are," he states, taking a step forward.

"What does our wings have to do with anything? Gabriel, stop with the mystery and just tell me!" I scream, the scream passing through the forest, the birds above reacting to the sound of my voice, the trees moving their branches.

"There are light and dark protectors. Your mate Damon is now a light protector. Your mate Daniel was light but now is a dark protector." He stops and looks at me.

"And me? What am I?" I ask in a quiet whisper.

"You, Sky…you are both…you are light and you are dark. One of the protectors' main powers is the ability to keep both Angels and demons in line," he states in a calm quiet voice.

"What does that even mean?" I say while shaking my head.

"It means, Sky, that you are more powerful than you realize. There have not been protectors for centuries. Now there are three," he states, finally closing the distance I have tried to create between us. I watch him lift his hand and place it on my shoulder. "That is why I sent Michael to protect you…watch over you…and guide you. We can't let any of you get into the hands of Barbas," he states as he takes a deep breath.

"What the hell am I supposed to do?" I yell at him.

Gabriel begins taking a few steps back from me. "Stay safe. All of you need to take care of one another."

Gabriel turns and starts walking away. "Wait! Where are you going?" I yell after him.

He doesn't stop but simply states, "To find more answers."

I watch him walk into the woods and disappear. I am now in the middle of the woods. I turn around and see Damon standing there, watching me; his breathing is steady, his eyes are locked on mine, his thoughts and emotions flooding into me once again, taking over.

CHAPTER 5

Trust Is Earned, Not Just Given

Damon

I try my best to control my thoughts and emotions, but I can't help it. I flood into her, grabbing onto her soul with mine; her eyes are locked on mine, mine on hers.

"Damon...," Sky states, searching my eyes. "How long have you been standing there?"

I take a deep breath. "Long enough, Sky," I state, trying to hide my anger, but I already know she knows my true feelings. I slowly make my way to her and open my arms. I wait patiently for her to take my invite and enter into my arms. She stands there for a moment and then finally gives into my gesture. she wraps her arms around my waist, and I wrap my arms around her as tightly as I can.

"I know why Barbas has been after us...why he has been after me," she states as she shoves her face into my chest.

"Sky, we know," I state.

"What? How? Oh...," she states, still having her face shoved in my chest. "Does Michael know?" she asks as she pulls her face away from my chest.

I shake my head. "No... I don't think so. I heard your thoughts when I was coming to find you," I state as calmly as I can.

I slowly let go of her. She takes a few steps back. "So what do we do now?" she asks.

17

"I don't know, Sky, but I think it's time for us both to go back to the cottage. You can talk to Michael there," I state, reaching out my hand to her. I watch her take a deep breath and grab my hand.

I have noticed that we all have gotten pretty good at taking deep breaths. I think it is the only thing we can do so we all don't fall apart.

Sky takes the lead, and we start walking down the path. "Sky, I know that this new information has us all confused, but we need to make sure we don't forget that we need to focus on finding the dagger. This new information might help us later on, but right now, it does nothing for us," I state as calmly as I can.

She continues to walk down the pathway, holding my hand tighter. "I know you are right, but I need to talk to Michael. I need to find out if he knew about this," she states, not hiding her anger.

Knowing now what we are and what she is has me a little nervous, because honestly, I have never heard of protectors before. I don't know what it means for our bond or with what we have to do in the future with Barbas.

We continue down the path and finally come to the opening to the field. I stop and Sky stops beside me, our hands still intertwined. "I love you, Sky," I state, looking at her.

She slowly turns her head and looks at me. "I love you, too, Damon," she states and turns back to look at the field. We can see the cottage from here, the fence, the place that we have all learned to call home. It has been our safe haven, but I don't know for how much longer it will stay that way.

Sky releases my hand and takes some steps into the field. The rain is still coming down, the clouds still rolling in, each set darker than the last; a storm is coming.

I watch her wait a moment, and then she begins to make her way through the field. I watch for a moment, and I follow behind her, allowing her to lead.

We come up to the wooden hidden door that I created. We both stop. I can hear Michael pacing back and forth, talking to himself. Sky takes a deep breath and puts her hand on the doorknob.

CHAPTER 6

We Are Only as Sick as Our Secrets

Michael

I have been waiting by the wooden door for a while now, waiting for Sky to return. I tried to stop Damon when he wanted to go look for her, but he would not listen to me. Their soul-bond continues to get stronger and deeper with every passing day.

I pace back and forth, waiting for her to return. I stop when I hear and see that the doorknob is beginning to turn. I can hear Damon's and Sky's breathing on the other side of the door. I watch her turn the doorknob and push the wooden door open. She stands there staring at me. I can see rage and confusion on her face and in her eyes.

Whatever happened in those woods has changed the way she looks at me; she looks as if I have betrayed her in some way. I see Damon standing behind her, waiting for her to take the steps needed to enter into the yard and out of the field.

After a few minutes of her and Damon just standing there looking at me, Sky finally takes the steps and enters into the yard and stands off to the side so Damon can enter as well. As soon as they are far enough from the door, I gently close the door and turn around and face Sky. I watch her look over at Damon and nod.

He nods back and heads up to the cottage. I wait to hear the door open and close.

"Sky, where have you been?" I ask in a concerned voice.

She stands there for a moment and then takes a step toward me. I watch her hands turn into fists.

"Did you know?" she asks.

"Know what?" I ask and watch her take another step forward. "Did you know that we are protectors?" she yells.

I shake my head. "No…no, I did not know."

"I don't believe you," she states as she takes another step forward. She is now only inches away from me; I can feel her rage in waves coming off of her.

I go to put my hand on her arm, but she quickly moves it out of my reach. "Sky, I promise you I didn't know. I told you that I was trying to find out more information, and I have been trying."

"Have you?" she states, not hiding her rage.

"Yes…who…who told you that you and your mates were protectors?" I ask, standing there, watching her.

She takes in a deep breath and tries to release it as slowly as she can. "Who do you think, Michael?"

I stand there, trying to piece the puzzle together in my head. I shake my head. "Gabriel…Gabriel told you, didn't he?"

She nods. "Yes, he did."

"What else did he tell you?" I ask as I watch her take a step back.

"Nothing. He wouldn't say anything else except that I have more power than I know."

"I'm sorry, Sky, I should have known as soon as I saw your wings, but I didn't piece it back together. You have to understand that protectors have not existed for centuries…," I state, watching her take yet another step back. I want to comfort her. I want to wrap her in my arms and plead with her, promise her that I didn't know any of this; but in this moment, the way she is looking at me tells me that nothing I say in this moment is going to take away her pain, her feelings that I have betrayed her.

"Michael, I have known you for centuries, and until recently, I have never questioned you…never thought that you would lie to me…or hurt me…but today, I can't say that anymore," she states, looking me in the eyes. Her eyes begin to fill with tears, and she allows them to escape from her eyes. I watch black and white tears run down her face.

"Sky, there are many secrets, many things that you do not know. I can't just tell you everything, but I know that nothing I tell you right now is going to change the fact that you are hurting. So all I can say is I am sorry," I state, taking a step back to make more distance between us.

Sky looks at me for a few more moments and slowly makes her way past me, not stopping, not saying one more word. I turn around to watch her head up to the cottage. I see Daniel standing in the window of the door, waiting for her to get closer so he can open the door and welcome her back. She stares at the ground, watching each step she takes.

She makes her way up to the door. She slightly turns around to look at me one more time, tears still escaping her eyes.

I hear her whisper, "We are only as sick as our secrets." And she turns back around, and Daniel opens the door and embraces her with a hug. I watch his arms open wide, and she enters them without question. She shoves her face into his chest; his arms wrap around her tightly.

In this moment, I am jealous of what they have with her. She loves them, she desires them, she is loyal to them.

I watch Daniel take some steps back, still holding her tightly in his arms. I see Damon walking up behind Daniel and Sky. He puts his hand on the door; his eyes connect with mine, then he slowly and calmly shuts the door, leaving me alone in the rain, longing to make things right with Sky.

I shake my head and look up at the sky, the rain falling down and hitting my face. There are many secrets I haven't told any of them—secrets about me, secrets about the dagger, and secrets about the waters of Edanya.

Sky's words echo in my mind, *We are only as sick as our secrets*. I look back to the cottage. I walk a few minutes and slowly make my way up. When I get to the door, I see Sky, Daniel, and Damon in the living room, all talking, all waiting for me to come in so we all can have a chat. I hope they are ready for the answers.

CHAPTER 7

Michael, Whose Side Are You On?

I have been sitting here, listening to my mates arguing, waiting for Michael to finally come in so we can talk. I look over to the back door and see Michael standing outside looking in. His eyes connect to mine.

I watch him turn the doorknob and push open the door. As soon as it swings open, both of my mates stop talking and turn and look at Michael.

Michael is standing there in the doorway, soaked. I watch him look at all of us. His eyes are searching ours; his eyes look tortured, heavy. His body is calm; his breathing is steady. After a few moments, he walks in from outside and closes the door behind him.

He slowly walks over to the fireplace and leans against the bricks. I look around the room and notice how we all have found our spots—the same spots that we have made our own since coming back to the cottage. Michael always leans against the bricks, Damon sits in the chair facing the fire, and Daniel and I both sit on the couch.

Daniel's eyes are burning into me. I know that he is waiting for me to speak, but my eyes are locked onto Michael's and his onto mine. "Tell us, Michael…tell us what you know," I state in a stern voice.

Michael nods. "As you already know, all three of you are protectors," he states, looking to me, then to my mates.

"Tell us something we don't already know," Daniel asks, putting his hand on my leg.

"There are light protectors and dark protectors. The light protectors watch over the Angels and the humans, including watchers, making sure that the light stays in balance. The dark protectors watch over the demons, witches, and the prince of darkness, making sure that the dark stays in balance." Michael stops and stares at me for a moment.

"You are telling me that there are witches, really?" Daniel asks, sounding amused.

"Yes, Daniel, there are many things about our world that you don't know and many things that neither Damon nor Sky knows. Our world is filled with secrets and mysteries," Michael states, looking at Daniel.

"And those that are both?" I ask. I feel Daniel squeeze my leg, all of us waiting to hear Michael's answer.

"Those of the protectors that are both—light and dark—they look over all, making sure that all of it—the light and the dark—stays within balance," Michael states, continuing to search my eyes.

"And that is me?" I state, trying to hide my nerves.

Michael nods. "Does this help us with finding the dagger?" I ask.

Michael shakes his head. "Yes and no. Yes, because you all have powers, powers that come over time. The soul-bond helps your powers get stronger. No, because you still need me to find the waters of Edanya, and we still need Argo to find the pieces."

"So for now, we do what? Continue waiting for Argo to show up?" Daniel asks, not hiding his irritation.

I put my hand on top of his hand and squeeze, trying to comfort him, trying to calm him down. His temper is different than I remember; he is a lot more unhinged, but now it is beginning to make sense. When they tried to change him into a demon, they brought forth his true nature, which was a protector; but because of them, his mark was changed, and now he is dark. With that comes his temper; the darkness is within him, whether I like it or not.

"Yes, we wait. It won't be long now. Barbas is not patient. If we now all know what you guys are, then you can bet he knew it when you were in hell, and nothing will stop him," Michael states, looking into the flames of the fire.

"We will stop him," Damon states.

I look over at Damon; he is staring into the fire. From the light from the fire, I can see his pure white markings in a different way. He is strong, courageous; he has transformed into a man that I am honored to be mated to. I used to fear him, I used to want to kill him, but now all I can do is be thankful that he is mine.

Damon looks from the fire to me.

"I hope you are all ready for what is going to be asked of you," Michael states.

"We will be," I state, continuing to look at Damon.

I look at Michael, who is staring at me once again. "Is there anything else you need to tell us?" I ask.

Michael shakes his head. "That is all for now. When the time is right, I will tell you all more."

Michael pushes off of the bricks and heads toward the back door. We all watch him as he walks away. He has always been good at riddles.

He doesn't turn around. He doesn't say another word. I watch him grab the doorknob, turn it, and push the door open. The rain is pouring now, the clouds above letting out their rage. Michael walks out the door. I slowly get up from the couch, Daniel taking his hand away from my leg. I walk over to the door and watch Michael head down the yard toward the wooden door. He doesn't waste any time getting down to the door, opening it, and walking into the field, closing the door behind him.

I stand there looking up at the sky. Even the rain I welcome since escaping hell. It is good to see anything that is not stone and brick, wooden doors, and lanterns. I turn my head slightly to look at my mates, both of them watching me. I turn my head back around and walk outside, closing the door behind me.

I can hear Damon's and Daniel's thoughts going wild, trying to make sense of what Michael just told us.

I look around the yard and see the bench down by the small wooden shed. I start making my way down to it, just needing time to think. Each step I take, my feet sink into the mud, the grass being overtaken by the mud that gives them life. I take the last few steps and take a seat on the wooden bench. I position myself so I can directly watch the wooden door. It is supposed to be a secret, but I am guessing by now, if Argo is watching the cottage, he knows that it is there, and when he finally gets the courage to enter, I will be here waiting for him.

CHAPTER 8

Looking into the Flames

Daniel

I watch Sky walk out the door. She closes it behind her. I watch her staring up at the sky. Everything about her draws me in. I hate when she decides to leave and make distance between us. Even though I can hear her, even though I can feel her, sometimes that is not enough. I need more; I want more.

I get up from the couch and take several steps toward the door.

"Daniel, just let her be," I hear Damon state.

I turn my head and look into his eyes. He is calm, balanced—everything I am not. "How are you not freaking out about what we just learned?" I ask.

Damon turns his eyes to the flames. "Everything will be okay, Daniel."

I turn my head back to the door. I take the last few steps. I put my hands against the door, and I look out the window and see Sky sitting on the bench, looking at the wooden door. She is going to wait until either Argo shows up or Michael returns; knowing her, probably both.

I back away from the door and put my hand on the doorknob. I can hear Damon's breathing; I can feel his eyes burning through me. "She should not be alone right now," I state as I turn the doorknob and push the door open. Sky looks at me. I stand there in the doorway. She doesn't stare for that long, maybe a few seconds, and then she turns her head back to the wooden door.

"Sky is never alone, Daniel…remember that," Damon states as I take a step outside and close the door behind me. Damon doesn't stand or try to stop me from going to her; he just continues to sit on the chair and look into the flames.

The rain quickly soaks my clothes and my hair. The wind is starting to pick up, the sky not hiding its anger. I start making my way to the bench. I look down at the ground as I slowly make my way to her. After a few moments, I get to where she is sitting. She doesn't look away from the wooden door. "Sky," I whisper and take a seat next to her. I put my hand on her leg and squeeze; this gesture has become our way of showing support to each other.

"Daniel, I am all right," she states, looking from the door to me. She leans in and connects our lips; she leans in deeper, getting as close as she can. I return the desire. She opens her mouth and allows me to enter, a gesture that she has not done in months.

After a few moments, she gently pulls away.

"Are you all right?" Sky asks me with concerns in her eyes.

I sit there for a moment, just her taking in—her eyes, her scent, her concern, her inner yearning for me. I nod. "Yes, I am all right… but worried," I whisper.

"I think we are all worried," she whispers back.

"Sky, I don't like any of these plans. I don't trust Michael, and I still don't trust Damon. I think we need to come up with a different plan. I don't like the idea of us putting you out in the open, just waiting for Argo to come. What if something goes wrong? What if you get hurt?" I state, not hiding my concern.

"You ask a lot of questions," Sky states, not hiding her amusement.

"Sky, I can't lose you. I can't be away from you again. I won't be able to survive it," I state.

She leans in and reconnects our lips again but only for a moment; she pulls away and brings her hands up and cups my face into her hands. "Daniel, you won't lose me. Everything is going to be okay," she states, lowering her hands down from my face.

I stand up from the bench, looking at the wooden door. I take a deep breath and turn and face her, her eyes watching my movement. "Why does everyone keep saying that everything is going to be okay?" I state in a stern voice.

I watch Sky stand and face me. "Because everything is going to be okay," she states.

"How can you be so certain, Sky? Every time I think that we have won, every time I think we are free, it turns out we are not," I state as my hands turn into fists.

Sky looks at the wooden door, and then looks at me again, searching my face. "Daniel, we have to keep going… We have to…," Sky states in a stern voice.

"Why, Sky? Why do we have to? We could just run away. We could hide away together," I state, trying to convince her and myself.

"Daniel, I can't, not after everything that has happened. We have to finish what we have started," she states in a calm voice.

I shake my head and run my hands through my hair. I take a step back from her. She stands there and just stares. "Sky," I whisper.

"I think you should go back to the cottage. I will stand watch out here," she states as she takes another step back and takes a seat once again on the bench and faces the wooden door.

I nod. I want to stay with her, I want to be with her, but I know by her thoughts and her emotions that she is okay. Even after all this time, I still take offense when she is fine with me, without her mates. If Damon feels at all the way I do. It appears, at times, it hurts us more to be away from her than it does for her to be away from us.

Maybe one day, I will ask her. I have noticed, since us being back on the surface, that parts of her are still guarded; she only allows me and Damon to access parts of her.

I turn and start heading back to the cottage. The rain is coming down harder now; the sun has gone down, and now the sky is dark, filled with the black cloud still releasing their anger onto the world. Nature is doing the only thing she can do—she is starting to defend herself.

I make my way up the yard and up to the door. I look into the window and see that Damon has not moved; he doesn't have to, for he knows what she is thinking and feeling, the same as I do.

I put my hand on the doorknob and turn it and push the door open. Slowly Damon looks from the fire to me, and back to the fire again. I take several steps inside and close the door behind me.

I take a deep breath and slowly make my way to the couch. I stop and look at the fire, the heat radiating off of the flames, replacing the coldness on my skin. I turn and take a seat on the couch.

Damon and I both look into the flames, waiting for our mate to come back inside.

CHAPTER 9

Watching Reveals More Than We Knew

Argo

It only took me a few days to shadow to England. I don't know what it is with this place that keeps them all coming back here, but from what I have observed so far, they have made it their home. I have watched Sky, Daniel, Damon, and Michael for about a day now, making sure that I stay hidden and in the shadows. The rumors must be due about what they are, because Damon hasn't come out of the cottage, and he doesn't appear to be sensing that I am here.

It is weird to see him the way he is now. As long as I have known him, he has always been claimed by the darkness. He was the prince for centuries, and now because of the soul-bond, he has changed; he is no longer the prince I knew or fought for or fought beside.

I can see that Sky is sitting on the wooden bench by the small shed, staring at the wooden gate. She has forgotten that we don't need to use doors. She is trying to prepare for my attack, thinking that I would make it that easy, that simple on them. I might still only be a demon, but I am not that stupid.

I see that Michael is coming out of the forest and heading back toward the wooden door. He looks tired and worn from up here. I haven't seen the other Angel yet, but one thing I have learned over the centuries is that Angels watch over their own, just like demons do. We do not allow our own to go somewhere completely alone.

I do the one thing my prince told me not to do—I allow the shadows to disappear. I walk out and in the open; I hide behind a tree, making sure that none of them have caught my scent. They have not reacted so far. I slowly come out from behind one tree and walk down closer to the small wooden shed, stopping behind another tree, listening, watching, observing.

I feel naked without the shadows. I take a deep breath and finally find the courage to get out from behind the tree. I can hear Sky and Michael talking more clearly now, not wanting to use any of my powers, in case the Angel can sense power.

I take another few steps and get behind another tree that is directly behind the wooden shed.

The rain is coming down harder than before, the thunder and lightning filling the sky above. Mother Earth is angry; she is trying to make a statement, and so far, she is not disappointing. I forget how alive she is and the power she wields. I forget that we have all tried to claim her, but in the end, she reminds us that she is not a slave.

I take another deep breath and come out from behind the tree. I take a few more steps and put my hands against the wooden fence and look between the small crack between the wooden shed and the fence that is trying to hang on. The fence is old, broken, barely able to hold onto the earth that has kept it up for a long time. I am surprised that Damon has not put up better defenses.

I can see now how just unprepared they really are; they are not concerned about me or Barbas. In this moment, they are only worried about themselves—about her.

Everything since Barbas has taken the prince of darkness's throne has been about her; everything that has happened recently has been centered around her, a woman of great power, power that none of us has ever seen. They call her the chosen one.

I take a step back from the fence and allow my hands to fall to my sides. I can feel someone watching me.

I turn around and immediately know who he is—the great Angel Gabriel. The stories about him does not do him justice.

CHAPTER 10

You Will Give Me What I Want

Gabriel

I am watching all of them: Michael and Sky are in the yard, Daniel and Damon are both in the cottage, and Argo is not far away, watching Michael and Sky from the fence. Michael is not aware that the demon is watching them. I have always told him to stay on guard, and for reasons I only know of, all of his attention is on her. The demon turns around when he finally feels my eyes on him. When he turns, he looks me over from head to toe; not many demons have seen Angels in person, not for centuries anyways.

I thought this demon would run when he felt me watching him, but instead he just turned around and his eyes met mine. He acts as if it is the normal thing to do when a demon is in the presence of an Angel, but it is not. This demon has courage and fearlessness about him. I can see now why Barbas sent him to watch over Sky, to watch over all of them; he will not turn away from a challenge like the others would.

"Why did you come out of the shadows? Didn't your master tell you what would happen?" I state, standing still and watching the demon. His eyes are not worried nor concerned; his eyes tell a different story—this demon is curious.

"He has told me many things, Angel of the light," Argo replies, not taking his eyes away from mine. I take a small step forward. He responds with taking a step backward. Smart demon, not wanting me to get too close to him.

I take another step forward and watch him back into the fence. As soon as his back hits the fence, Michael and Sky stop talking. I can hear their footsteps and them opening the wooden door and coming over to where I am standing in front of the demon.

I look over at Sky and Michael as they get closer. Sky stops when she sees Argo.

"I can't believe he actually came," she states in a low whisper.

I look to Michael; his eyes are locked onto the demon. I look back over to Sky and watch her take a step forward toward the demon. She doesn't get very far when Michael grabs her arm, keeping her in place.

I look back to the demon; his eyes are looking from them to me. "What are you going to do, Angel? Kill me? I am not afraid of death," he states, trying to hide his curiosity.

I didn't try to hide my amusement as I allowed a smirk to escape my lips. I take another step forward. "Oh, demon, that would be too easy. Of course we are not going to kill you. In fact, we need you alive." As the words leave my lips, I watch the demon's eyes go wide.

"Tell us where it is!" Sky yells at the demon.

I hear the door at the cottage open and shut, and hear four footsteps quickly making their way to us. Daniel and Damon could not stay away any longer. Their need to be with her is stronger than I thought, and it appears that it is also rubbing off on Michael; his hand is still gripping her arm. I am surprised she has not pulled away from his touch.

It doesn't take Daniel and Damon long until they are both on either side of Sky. Michael tightens his hold on her arm. By the look on Daniel's and Damon's faces, they do not approve of his gesture toward Sky but doesn't try to intervene.

"Where is it?" Sky states again, locking her eyes with the demon's. I watch him look her up and down.

"All of this for you?" the demon states with anger in his voice.

Damon takes a step forward, his eyes filled with rage; his voice is low. "Answer the question, Argo."

Argo looks back to me. "I can't," is all he can say.

Daniel takes a step forward. "Wrong answer, demon."

"He will kill me... I can't," the demon states, his eyes pleading.

I take another step forward, leaving only about a foot between the demon and me. "One way or another, you will give us what we want."

The demon doesn't say anything; he just watches and waits for whatever is about to happen. One thing I can promise is that he will not be ready for this.

I look over to Michael, who is still gripping Sky's arm, trying to keep her from going to the demon. "Michael, you can let go of her. The demon will not harm her," I state, waiting for him to look at me.

"How can you say that?" Daniel states, taking a step toward me.

"Because I am here, the demon will not harm any of you," I state, trying to hide my irritation.

I watch Michael take in a deep breath and gently release his hold on her arm. Sky doesn't look at him but continues to look at the demon.

"Michael, will you please come here?" I ask, looking at him, looking at her.

He slowly makes his way to my side. "We need to bring him into the fenced yard by the small wooden shed." Michael nods and doesn't say anything. He makes his way over to the demon that tries to back up again but can't; the fence will not allow him.

He stands to the side of the demon; the demon looks at Michael. "You can come on your own, or I can force you. The choice is yours, demon," he states in a calm tone.

The demon stands there looking from Michael to me, and back to Michael again, Sky, Daniel, and Damon watching him closely. "I will go," the demon states.

Michael goes to grab his arm, but the demon quickly pulls it away. "I said that I would go... I can walk on my own!" the demon yells.

Michael stands still for a moment, then slowly leans in closer to the demon. "Watch your tone, demon. We need what is in your mind, remember that. Your limbs are not off-limits." Michael pulls back.

"What are we going to do with him? We have to find out where he put the pieces," Daniel states.

"We will put him in the blue flame," I state, looking over to Sky. Her eyes meet mine.

"What the hell is the blue flame?" Daniel asks, getting more annoyed.

"You will see, young protector," I state and nod to Michael.

CHAPTER 11

Orders Are Orders When They Come from Him

Michael

I stand there waiting for the demon to finally take steps toward me and follow as he has been told. I watch him breath in and out, in and out; he is trying to hide his fear, but now the scent is radiating off of him. He can't hide it, even if his words say he is not afraid. I slightly turn and look at Sky, Damon, and Daniel. They nod and back away. I turn back to the demon, who is now watching Sky, Damon, and Daniel walk over to Gabriel, all of them watching him as much as he is watching them.

"Come, demon, let's get this over with," I state. The demon takes a few steps toward me. Gabriel watches the demon. I turn around and start walking about the fence toward the wooden door that is now no longer hidden. I hear several footsteps behind me. I slightly turn around and see the demon not far behind me, and Sky, Daniel, and Damon behind him. Gabriel is in the back, watching all of us. He has always been the purest of us all, watching and protecting.

The rain has continued to pour down, and by the looks of the sky, she doesn't plan on stopping anytime soon. Her wrath is being felt around the world tonight; she is angry and becoming unhinged.

I continue to make my way to the wooden door. I can feel all their eyes on me, burning through me. Gabriel thinks highly of me; sometimes I think he thinks too highly of me, he thinks that I can do anything, but I would never admit to him that I am a little afraid. Controlling the blue flame is hard, and once it is started, the only way it goes out is once the demon gives up the information we are seeking. The blue flame does as we command it; with no question, it is loyal to a fault when it comes to the pure Angels.

We finally come to the door. I put my hand on the doorknob and can hear the demon taking deep breaths behind me. I can feel Sky's, Daniel's, and Damon's heartbeats racing like horses in the wild. I turn the doorknob and push the door open. I walk through it and take several steps into the yard. When I turn around, the demon is at the opening, looking into the yard, not wanting to pass through the barrier.

I can tell that Daniel is getting impatient because he doesn't waste any more time on the demon and pushes him through the doorway. As soon as he does, the wind begins to pick up; the trees begin to sway. I watch Daniel, Damon, and Sky look around.

"What is that?" Sky asks in a whisper.

"Protection," I state as I watch the demon take a few more steps into the yard. Sky, Damon, and Daniel make their way through the doorway, and Gabriel behind them, all of them taking enough steps for the door to close.

Michael makes his way over to my side. Sky is standing off to the side; Damon and Daniel are each by her side, watching the demon.

"Go behind the demon, and I will stand in front of him," Gabriel orders.

I nod and make my way behind him, standing only about a foot away. Gabriel stands in front of him. We both slowly kneel to the ground, placing our hands on Mother Earth. We both close our eyes. After a few moments, we both open our eyes, our eyes glowing bright blue; the ground begins to shake, the wind becomes more uncontrolled, the trees swinging back and forth. I look up to the demon and see him looking around, trying to keep his balance.

After a few moments, the ground stops shaking, the wind slows down, and the trees go back to their original place. A circle begins to form around the demon, getting brighter and brighter with each passing second. Soon flames begin to emerge from the ground, increasing in size and height. The demon stands still. The flames get higher and higher until the demon is imprisoned in a dome of blue flames. Gabriel and I slowly begin to stand, our eyes turning back, the glow getting dimmer and dimmer until there is no evidence of any change at all.

Gabriel and I both slowly back away from the blue flames. I make my way gently over to Sky, Damon, and Daniel; Gabriel remains standing in front of the demon.

The demon begins to scream; the scream echoes through the yard and into the forest. Sky tries to take a step forward, but I grab her arm before she can take one step. She looks at me, her eyes searching my face.

"Let it be," I whisper to her. She nods and looks back at Gabriel and the demon. I release her arm, and I look over to Gabriel.

"You will give us what we want, demon," Gabriel states as he kneels back down to the ground. Gabriel lowers his hands to the ground. At first nothing happens, then the ground begins to shake again. Sky grabs my arm, trying to keep balanced, a gesture that I welcome from her. After everything I have put her through, I never thought she would forgive me.

Slowly, from the ground, blue-flamed chains start to come up. The demon continues to scream, unable to move or escape. The chains begin to wrap around his ankles, then continues up until it wraps around his wrists; one single flame continue to go up until it wraps around his neck.

"I will not give you what you seek!" the demon screams.

I watch Gabriel shake his head. "Demons, they are so stubborn. I admire your courage, young demon. The flames, on the other hand, will not. The chains holding you are not so admiring. Be careful, demon."

Gabriel gently stands up from the ground. The flames slowly turn dark blue. I watch Gabriel turn around and face us. "We will take shifts watching him. In due time, he will give us what we want." Gabriel looks at each of us and turns toward the wooden door. We all watch him take a deep breath and slowly make his way to the wooden door.

"Where are you going?" Sky asks.

Gabriel doesn't turn around but simply states as I watch him put his hand on the doorknob, "Not far. I will be watching." He turns the doorknob and pushes the door open.

The field is dark, the rain still pouring down from the clouds. The forest is still. He begins taking small steps into the field.

Daniel takes a deep breath and walks over to the wooden door. "He is just leaving?"

"No, he is waiting. The demon will give in. The flames always get what they want," I state as calmly as I can.

"And what is that?" Daniel states, beginning to close the door.

"The truth, young protector, the truth," I state.

Sky releases her hold on my arm. I watch her take several steps toward the demon. Damon takes a step forward, watching her.

"I will take the first watch," Sky states, taking another few steps.

"I will stay with you," Daniel states, closing the door.

I watch Sky make her way over to the bench. She takes a seat facing the demon. "The rest of you should go into the cottage. We don't all have to be out here," Sky whispers.

"Very well. Damon, you will take the next watch after Sky and Daniel," I state as I start making my way up to the cottage. Damon follows, not saying a word.

CHAPTER 12

We Can't Wait Forever

Daniel

I stand there still facing the wooden door. I slowly lean into the wooden door and rest my forehead against it. I take a few deep breaths and lift my head from the wooden door and slowly turn around to face Sky. She is not looking at me; she is looking at the demon. His screams have started to decrease. He hasn't tried struggling as of yet. I take a few steps toward the demon, making sure that he can see me as clearly as I can see him.

Not that long ago, I was the one in chains and being tortured, and he was the one guarding me, ordering his men to torture me. His eyes are locked onto mine. I take another step forward. I can hear Sky not that far away, still sitting on the bench, taking in a deep breath. She is trying to prepare herself for whatever I am about to do.

"Looks like we have changed places. How does it feel to be the one in chains?" I ask him, not hiding the amusement in my voice. I allow for a small smirk to escape my lips. The demon doesn't move; his eyes remain locked onto mine.

"You will get yours again, Daniel. Don't worry about that!" Argo screams.

I take another step forward. "In due time, we will see, Argo. Just give up, Tell us where the pieces are," I state, putting my hands into fists. Sky stands up from the bench and slowly makes her way over to me. I turn to face her. She puts both of her hands on my chest. I take a deep breath.

"Daniel, he is trying to get to you. Don't let him," she whispers as she leans in and gently connects our lips. I lean into her, wanting more, needing more.

Our desire and passion is short-lived when the demon starts screaming once again, the screams echoing through the yard and into the forest. Birds fly from their nests; the thunder and lightning responds with its own scream.

Sky drops her hands from my chest and takes a step back. "Daniel, we are to watch him. That is all, leave it be," she states as she turns around and cautiously makes her way back to the wooden bench. I watch as Argo's eyes follow her. His sights are no longer set on me, but now it is set on her.

I take several steps toward Sky. I watch her sit back down and face the demon; both of their eyes are locked onto each other.

"Do you like pain that much, or do you just spite us that much to where you would rather endure the pain from the flames instead of telling us what we want to know?" Sky asks as her hands begin to form into fists.

The demon doesn't say anything at first. "Actually neither, Sky. What you are asking me to do, I physically can't do."

"What do you mean? Just say the words, and all of this will be over," she states, her voice getting louder.

I look at the demon and wait for him to respond. I still think this is all a waste of time. We need to know where the pieces are, and doing it the Angels' way is taking too long. My patience is running thinner and thinner with each passing moment. I am done playing their game. The demon will never give us what we want. He will always do exactly what Barbas wants him to do; that will never change.

"I mean that I have to follow what the prince demands. I can't go against him. He told me I can't tell anyone—" the demon yells in pain.

I take another step toward Sky. "He is just playing games with us, Sky. He is never going to tell us anything. We should just kill him," I state, continuing to look at the demon.

I watch Sky slowly stand up from the bench and face me; her hands are still in fists, her thoughts and emotions getting louder, more uncontrolled. "We can't kill him, Daniel. He is the only one that knows where the pieces are. We need the dagger in order to kill Barbas, remember?"

"Maybe there is another way. Maybe we can figure out another way to kill Barbas without having to play these games," I state, trying to keep my own thoughts and emotions under control.

Sky shakes her head and faces the demon again. "We need the dagger, Daniel. Even if it takes more time, we need to stay this course." I watch her gently sit back down onto the wooden bench.

No one is going to listen to what I have to say. Sky and Damon are going to listen to Gabriel and Michael. I take in a deep breath and do my best to release it as slow as I can. I turn around and walk toward the small wooden shed. The rain is still coming down; the sky is still angry. Mother Earth appears to be as unhinged as the rest of us.

I get to the shed and lean my shoulder against it, positioning myself so I can see the demon, Sky, and the wooden door. Gabriel can't watch from the distance forever. This was his plan; he needs to make sure that it works out the right way.

"What did you mean when you said you must follow? I have seen demons go against the prince before, so why can't you?" I hear Sky calmly ask the demon.

"I am different," the demon states back.

"How? Why?" Sky asks.

"Because I am the prince's right-hand man. I have been a part of the higher order for centuries. When I got my powers, I made a blood oath that I would obey and follow the prince of darkness, no matter what. Because I made the oath, my body, my brain will not let me disobey, even if I want to," the demon states in pain.

Sky doesn't respond but just continues to watch the demon, waiting for Gabriel to return, all of us waiting.

CHAPTER 13

The Cracks Are Starting to Show

One day later

It has been about a day since Gabriel and Michael put Argo the demon into the blue flames; the chains have gotten tighter with each passing hour. The demon still refuses to give us the information we want, and Gabriel has not returned from wherever he decided to go to. Damon and Michael have been waiting in the cottage. I can hear Damon's thoughts loud and clear; he is wanting to change places with Daniel. Their need to both want to be with me at any given time has not changed, and oddly enough, I have been beginning to see the same traits in Michael. He is wanting to talk to me more; he is wanting to be around me more.

The demon is still in pain and still lets out screams, not as often as he did at the beginning. Daniel is still leaning against the small wooden shed, watching the wooden door, watching the demon, and of course, still watching me.

"Daniel, why don't you go inside?" I state, watching him breathe.

"I am fine," he states, looking from the demon to me.

"Please...if Damon has to stay in that cottage any longer, he is going to go insane," I state in a pleading voice.

I watch Daniel push off of the small wooden shed and make his way to me. He doesn't waste any time closing the distance between us. Before I know it, he is standing in front of me, still wet from the

43

rain. His hair is in his face. In this light, he is looking downright sexy, which does not help my cause of wanting him to switch places with Damon.

I watch him breath in and out, and slowly, he leans down to meet me at my level and slowly connects our lips; it is soft, loving, kind, but also has a dark desire behind it. After a few seconds, I pull away; our eyes lock for a moment. Daniel takes in another deep breath, stands up straight, and starts making his way to the cottage.

Daniel gets to the cottage door, and I can hear him open the door, and just as soon as he does, I hear footsteps heading my way. I slightly turn around and see Damon coming straight at me. His eyes are locked on mine; a desire, a longing is radiating from him. His thoughts are loud; his emotions are going wild.

He closes the distance between us very quickly. He stands in front of me, taking in deep breaths. I stand up and lean into him. His arms wrap around me; my own arms wrap around his waist. Damon pulls me into him. Our lips connect in no time; his kiss, however, is rough, demanding, passionate. After a few minutes, Damon slowly pulls away and releases his grip around me. I allow my hands to fall to my sides.

Damon turns around and faces the demon. "He hasn't given you anything?" Damon asks.

"No, not yet. He says he can't," I state, trying to hide my anger.

"Well, Sky, for once, he is not lying. The blood oath the demons take is very powerful. They say it comes from very old magic. It can't be broken," Damon states, looking from the demon to me.

I search his face, his eyes. I know that what he states is true. Just in this moment, I don't want to believe it. I want to believe that there is some hope in us finding the pieces and being able to put the dagger back together again. Hope is all I have right now.

"So what do we do, Damon? If he can't tell us, then how are we supposed to find the pieces?" I state, trying not to yell.

He takes a step closer to me, so close that his chest is now against my chest. I can feel his breathing. I can feel his warmth from his body; his scent surrounds me. He leans into me, his mouth right by my ear. "We wait, Sky. Remember, nothing is what it appears to be."

He gently backs away from me, but before he can get too far away, I grab his arm. He stops; he looks down at my hands around his arm and then slowly looks up and looks into my eyes.

"Damon…"

"Sky," he whispers.

"Something about all of this doesn't feel right," I whisper back.

He studies my face and then glances over at the demon, then looks back at me. He slowly brings his free arm up, and his hand connects to my cheek. "Don't worry, Sky. I will not let anything happen to you. I love you, Sky," he whispers gently.

I take in a deep breath. "After everything that has happened… after everything that came out in the levels…your love hasn't changed, has it?" I ask in a quiet whisper.

His eyes are soft, warm, comforting. He drops his hand from my cheek and leans in again to where his lips are right by my ear. "My feelings for you are eternal, Sky. There is nothing in the world that would change that. We all have a dark side." He gently pulls back again.

I release his arm. I watch him walk to the wooden bench and take a seat facing the demon. I take a deep breath and follow his lead. I get to the bench and sit next to him. He slowly puts his hand onto my leg, both of us staring at the demon, him staring back.

This is going to be a lot harder than what I thought. This demon is stronger. I thought by now, he would give into the blue flames; but now that Damon has stated why the demon can't tell us, I have no idea what we are waiting for. Every moment that goes by gives Barbas more time to prepare and attack us if he wanted.

I know that my mates can read my thoughts and feel my emotions. So right now I know that my fear thoughts are flooding into them. I take a deep breath and return Damon's kind gesture; I put my hand on his leg, and we both wait.

CHAPTER 14

The Pain Is Just the Beginning

Argo

I stand here in the middle of the blue-flamed cage it has created around me, bound by dark-blue flamed chains. I can't escape even if I tried, but at this point, I am not trying. The chains are starting to dig into my flesh, leaving behind forever scars to remind me of what happened to me. The flames are slowly entering into me, causing me a pain that I have never felt before.

These flames don't care that I am a demon, but they are dead set on making sure that I give up the information the Angel wants me to. Like me, the flames are their slave, doing their bidding, even if we don't want to. I can't speak of where the pieces are, that much I am telling the truth, but what they don't know is I can pass on to Sky where I put the pieces because she has the abilities of seeing my past.

Eventually Damon or the Angels will figure this out, but until then, I am going to hold back as long as I can. Maybe I will even be the one to tell her how to get the information she seeks. I stand here in pain, in the flames, and can't take my eyes off of Sky and Damon. The way they are together is somewhat of a mystery to me. She acts differently with each mate. With Daniel, she is more guarded, cautious; with Damon, she appears to be more open, more passionate with him.

She might not see this difference, but I do, and I can tell by how Daniel acts when others are around; he can tell the difference as well. It has to be hard for all three of them loving her and her loving them both.

"Are you going to say something, Argo?" I hear Damon state. I watch him squeeze Sky's leg, a comforting gesture, one that I have not seen him show before. I look at Damon and see just how much he really has changed and not just because of the mark he wears or that we all now know that he is a light protector; it is something else. His eyes—behind them is love, passion, desire, longing, things that he lost when he became the prince of darkness. I look at Sky, and she is watching Damon, her eyes filled with wonder, trust, longing.

"What happened to you?" I state, gritting my teeth, trying my hardest to keep the scream from escaping my lips. The longer I hold out, the more the blue flames inflict its power upon me and, with it, great pain.

"A lot," Damon states, looking at Sky, and then looking at me again.

"It was her, wasn't it? The soul-bond did all of this to you?" I ask.

I watch him nod. "That is part of it, yes, but I think it was also when the soul-bond took hold, it awoke the true power within me, awoke who I really was all along but just couldn't see it through the darkness that took over me."

"And Daniel? What happened to him?" I ask in a curious voice.

"I believe it was the same for him in a way. It does all have to do with Sky," he states as he looks at her and leans in for a small quick kiss. I watch her lean into his touch, then just as quickly, he pulls away and looks at me.

"The real question is what happened to you, Argo?" Damon asks with concern in his voice, concern like he actually cares what happens to me. *Lies*, I tell myself. He doesn't care about me, not really; his only concern is her and killing Barbas. Everything else is just a means to get what he wants.

"You, Damon, you are what happened to me. You left me—you left all of us—for what? For her?" I scream as I try and move; the more I try and move, the tighter the chains become.

"That is not how it happened, and you know it… I never meant to leave you…or them. It just happened, Argo," Damon states, squeezing Sky's leg.

"You chose her. You could have walked away. You could have chosen us—chose me, your right-hand man, your best friend. But no, you chose her instead. You chose the love instead, and now look at you. You're not the prince. You're not even a demon anymore. You are a light protector!" I scream.

Damon takes his hand from Sky's leg and slowly stands up from the bench. He takes a step toward me. "Argo, I am sorry. I never meant for any of this to happen," Damon states.

I look into his eyes and can see the pain, the regret in his eyes. "It doesn't matter now, Damon. Nothing can undo what has been done. You are who you are, and I must serve the new prince," I state in a quiet whisper.

Damon takes a deep breath. I look over at Sky; she is bringing her hand up to Damon's arm. Damon looks over at Sky. He takes another deep breath and takes a step back and gently sits back down on the bench.

Damon reaches over and grabs Sky's hand. Sky looks at me. She doesn't say anything; she just takes a few deep breaths and continues keeping guard.

"It has to be hard, sharing her with another mate," I state, trying anything to bring out the old him.

"Not as hard as you may think," Damon states in a calm tone.

"With more time that passes, I promise you, it will become harder for all of you, but especially for her," I state in almost a whisper.

"If I were you, I would focus on your own problems and not Sky's. She is not the one in chains and imprisoned by blue flames," Damon states in an amused voice.

"You are right. I am imprisoned, but so is she. She just doesn't know it yet," I state as the chains dig a little deeper into my skin. I know my words sting him even if it's just a little, but one thing that hasn't changed is Damon's pride and ego; he will never let me see his pain.

I don't know how much longer I will be able to hold out until I give in and tell her my secret, but I know that once he finds out that I have told, he will kill me. Barbas holds nothing back when it comes to him feeling that he has been betrayed.

I look at the wooden door, not wanting to look at Damon's and Sky's eyes anymore. I will wait for the Angel Gabriel to return, just as they do.

CHAPTER 15

Just Give Them What They Want

Damon

Many words have been stated, and none of the words are the answers that we are seeking. We are all becoming more unhinged, and Argo is going to hold out for as long as he can.

"I think I should go get Michael. He has been waiting for his turn," I state as I lean into Sky and quickly lay a kiss on her lips. Before she can lean into my touch, I pull away and stand up from the bench. Sky watches my every move. "Don't talk to him, okay? Just watch him and watch the wooden door for Gabriel to return," I state, watching her eyes. She nods. I take a deep breath and look at Argo one last time.

Argo is looking at the wooden door, refusing to look into my eyes again. I begin taking steps toward the cottage. I can feel the tension in the cottage without even opening the door. Daniel is going insane in there, waiting for his turn to go back and watch with Sky. Since he has turned dark, his patience and emotions have been everywhere.

I get to the back door of the cottage. Michael is waiting, and opens the door for me. I stop and look at him; he looks as tired as we do.

"It is your turn to watch with her and watch Argo. He is trying to play games and get into our heads. Don't let him get into yours," I state as I watch him nod. He walks past me and heads down to the wooden bench to sit by Sky.

I close the door and wait for him to sit next to her; he does. I watch Sky give him a simple but kind smile, and they both look at Argo.

I turn and face the living room. Daniel is pacing back and forth in front of the fire. I watch him run his hands through his hair.

"Daniel," I state, trying to get his attention, but he doesn't stop or respond; he just keeps pacing back and forth. I take a deep breath and take a few steps toward him. "Daniel!" I yell. He finally stops and looks at me. "What are you doing?" I ask, confused by the tension in the room.

I watch as Daniel's hands turn into fists. He takes a small step forward; his eyes are tortured, filled with rage. "Why would you leave her with him?" Daniel states.

I stand there, not knowing what to say. I take another deep breath and take another step toward him. "It was his turn," I state in a calm tone.

I watch Daniel take a deep breath. "We can't trust him, Damon. We need to make sure we are watching him," Daniel states.

"Daniel, Sky will be fine with Michael. We can hear her thoughts and feel her emotions. If for some reason, she starts to feel uncomfortable, we will know, and we both can go to her. We can't be around her all the time. She needs space to breathe," I state, watching Daniel.

"Why is it that I am the only one that thinks he is not telling us everything?" Daniel yells.

I watch him go to the couch and sit down. He puts his hands on his knees and stares into the fire.

"You are not the only one, Daniel, but we need him. We have to try and get along," I state, making my way to the chair. I slowly sit down and face the fire. This is beginning to be a habit for us—sitting here and staring into the fire, waiting.

"We don't need him. There has to be another way. I don't want him anywhere near Sky, and with you also being her mate, you

51

should feel the same way, Damon," Daniel states, continuing to look into the fire.

"The mark has really changed you, hasn't it, Daniel?" I state, looking from the fire to Daniel, who is now staring at me.

"What do you mean?" Daniel whispers.

"I mean before the black mark, you were calmer, kind, gentle, and now you are more angry and unhinged, and not to mention jealous. I thought it was just with me, but now I see it is not," I state, watching his hands turn into fists again.

"A lot has changed, Damon, and I am not the only one. You have as well. Somehow you and I have changed places. You are the good one, and now I am the evil one," Daniel whispers.

I shake my head. "You are not evil, Daniel. You are a dark protector, and I am a light protector. You will get used to your new immortality soon enough and all the power that comes with it."

Daniel stares at me for a moment and then turns and looks back at the fire. "We all have new powers, but none of us know what the power is. I bet Michael knows, and he is holding the information for himself," Daniel states while shaking his head.

"Michael really gets under your skin that much, huh?" I state, looking from Daniel, back to the fire.

"Yes... Yes, Damon, he does. Doesn't he get under yours?" Daniel asks.

"No, not really. I have nothing to be jealous about. I know how Sky feels about both you and me. Nothing else matters," I state, taking in a deep breath.

"You are a better man than I, Damon," Daniel states.

I look from the fire back to Daniel. "We are both better men, Daniel. We are not perfect, but we do the best we can when it comes to Sky. It is not easy for any of us with her, with sharing her, but I know that her love is true."

"I still don't trust him," Daniel states, looking from the fire to me.

"And you may never will, but we do need him. He knows where the water of Edanya is, and we need him to lead us there. Remember why we are doing all of this—to get the pieces, put it back together again, and defeat Barbas," I state calmly.

Daniel nods and looks back at the fire. I do the same. There is something peaceful about the fire and the flames.

I take a deep breath and wait for it to be my turn to go back to Sky.

CHAPTER 16

How Much Pain Can One Demon Take?

Sitting here in the rain with Michael, watching the demon is more peaceful than what I thought it would be. I know that sounds strange, but being next to Michael brings forth a calmness that I can't exactly explain. He has always been calm, balanced. He doesn't try and start a conversation with me. Instead, we both sit here on the bench, watching the demon and watching the wooden door, waiting for Gabriel to return. Gabriel knows more than what he is telling any of us. He has always been good at keeping secrets and speaking in confusing riddles.

Argo doesn't seem that he is any closer to giving us what we want. If anything, he seems to be withdrawing even more, barely even talking anymore. He lets out his screams. But after, he goes silent, staring at us as we stare at him. I take a deep breath and look over at Michael. He is staring at the demon; his hands are on his knees. He is ready for anything that takes places, positioned in such a way that he can get up from the bench to intervene if need be.

"Are we ever going to talk to one another, or are we going to continue to sit in silence?" I ask in a whisper.

I watch Michael look from the demon to me, his eyes searching my face, then looking straight into my eyes, searching for something. I look right back at him, trying to find what he is hiding behind his eyes, but I can't. He has gotten good at hiding what he doesn't want others to see.

"I don't know what you want me to say, Sky. Everything has changed so much. All of this is new to me, as much as it is new to you," Michael states, continuing to look into my eyes.

"I don't know what to say either, Michael. None of us asked for any of this," I state, finally breaking our eye contact and looking over at the wooden door. "Does he know more than what he has told us, Michael?" I ask, continuing to look at the wooden door.

I hear Michael clear his throat and take in a deep breath. "Probably. Gabriel always knows more than what he states."

"Yes, he does. I just can't figure out what his end game is. He has always been such a mystery. He never lets any of us close enough," I state, slowly looking away from the wooden door. I turn my head and look at the demon, who is listening to every word we state.

I stare into his demon eyes and see pain, torment, and oddly enough, I also see desire and hope. I shake my head.

"What is it, Sky?" Michael states, a little confused.

"His eyes," I whisper.

Michael looks over at Argo and then back to me again, "What about them?"

"They are confusing. I swear I can see hope and desire in his eyes," I whisper.

Michael looks at Argo again. Argo's eyes are still on me, paying no mind to the Angel looking at him.

"There are many things in my eyes, Sky," Argo states, trying not to scream in pain.

"What do you mean?" I state, watching his eyes go from me to Michael, then back to me again.

"You will have to see. It's not time yet, but the time is coming, Sky," Argo states in an amused voice.

"Sky, don't listen to him. He is just trying to play more games. Wait and you will see that Gabriel always gets what he wants," Michael states as he puts his hand on my leg.

For a moment I thought I felt that same hot sensation I feel whenever I touch Daniel and Damon, but it can't be; that feeling only comes when I touch one of my mates, or they touch me. Michael is not my mate. I shake my head.

"I think that we are all playing games, Michael," I state, looking over at him.

"Some games are meant to be played, Sky. We all have to play one way or another. Sometimes we can't help but play along," Michael states calmly.

"I am sick of playing games," I state as I look back at Argo.

Michael doesn't say anything, but I can feel him looking at me. I hear Daniel tell me to be careful. Damon is silent, but I can tell that he is with me, observing, listening.

"Gabriel has been keeping secrets from you, too, hasn't he?" I ask Michael, still looking at Argo.

I can feel Michael take a deep breath. I slowly turn and look at him and watch him release the breath. Michael doesn't look at me; instead, he looks at the wooden door that Gabriel walked out of.

"Yes, he is keeping secrets from me as well. We are all keeping secrets, Sky," Michael states, turning his eyes to me.

"I am sick of everyone keeping secrets, but you are right. We all have secrets, things that we keep hidden away inside ourselves," I whisper, looking at Michael.

I hear the door of the cottage open. I look past Michael and see Daniel and Damon standing in the doorway, both of them eager to get out of the cottage. I nod at them; both of them smile and take several steps outside. Daniel closes the cottage door.

I watch them both start making their way down to the wooden bench that Michael and I have been sitting on. I look back to Michael and watch him take a deep breath in. Our alone time is over.

Michael takes his hand from my knee and drops it to his side.

"Has anything changed?" Daniel asks.

"No, everything is still the same. No answers yet," I state quietly.

I watch Daniel go to the small wooden shed and lean his shoulder against it like he has done before, positioning himself to watch the demon, the wooden bench, and the wooden door.

I look over at Damon, and he is making his way to me. He gets to the bench and takes a seat next to me—Damon on one side, and Michael on the other.

CHAPTER 17

This Is How It Has to Be

Michael

Being able to talk to Sky alone for a while was nice, but once again, her mates couldn't stay away for that long. I look over at Daniel; he is leaning against the wooden shed, watching the demon in the blue flames. His eyes slowly connect with mine, but it doesn't last long; he disconnects our stare and looks back at the demon.

"So how long are we supposed to wait for that Angel to come back from wherever he went?" Daniel asks, not hiding his anger.

"We will wait for however long it takes. I can't control the blue flame by myself, so even if we wanted to do something, we can't," I state, trying to keep my own emotions under control. Normally I am calm and balanced, but there is something about Daniel that makes me unhinged. He talks to me with no respect and looks at me like I am an outcast, and he definitely doesn't like it that I am getting closer to Sky.

"Daniel, we need to wait, and we all need to stay and be on the same side, okay?" Sky states, putting her hand on my leg. I watch Daniel watch her hand go onto my leg. His hands start to form into fists. Sky is looking at Daniel, and he is looking at her.

One thing I have learned about Sky, Daniel, and Damon is that all three are them are alphas, and none of them are willing to back down. This is going to make for a very interesting journey.

"We have been waiting, Sky. The longer we wait, the more prepared Barbas becomes, and we have no idea what he is planning," Daniel states, looking directly at Sky, then to the demon.

"I know what he is planning," the demon states in a low whisper.

We all look at the demon. He is looking directly at Sky.

"And let me guess, you can't tell us that either," Daniel states, looking from the demon to me.

"Actually I can, but I choose not to. The only person I will tell is Sky," the demon states with an amused voice.

"More games?" Sky whispers, looking into the demon's eyes.

"No games, Sky. I will only tell you," the demon states while allowing for a smirk to escape his lips.

"No, no, no. We are not leaving you here with him by yourself!" Daniels yells.

"If you want to know what Barbas's plan is with Sky, then you are going to have to trust me," Argo states.

"Trust you? You're kidding, right? You are the one that tortured me!" Daniel screams.

"Correction, I gave the order for you to be tortured. I never put my hands on you, Daniel," Argo states in a calm voice.

I watch Daniel push off of the small wooden shed; his hands are in fists. I drop my hand from Sky's knee. She calmly stands up and takes several steps toward Daniel.

"This will solve nothing. Both of you, stop it. Daniel, we need to know his plans. Even if I don't like it, we have to listen to the demon," Sky states in almost a yell at Daniel.

Daniel looks from the demon to Sky, and states, "I am not going back into that cottage."

I watch Sky take a deep breath and take another step toward Daniel; he takes several steps toward her at the same time, closing the distance between them. He gets close enough to where Sky is able to put her hands on his chest.

"Daniel, you don't have to go back inside. Why don't all of you go into the field, then you guys will be close in case something happens," Sky states calmly.

"Fine," Daniel states and backs away from Sky.

"Sky, be careful, and no matter what you do, don't touch him. You understand?" I state in a stern voice.

I watch her nod. Damon stands up from the bench and makes his way to the wooden door. Daniel takes a deep breath and makes his way to the wooden door. I look over at Sky, and she turns around to face me. I look into her eyes and see no fear, just determination.

I nod and make my way to the wooden door as well. Damon grabs and then turns the doorknob and pushes the door open. Damon walks through first, then Daniel, and then I do. I turn around and look at Sky and then look at the demon, and slowly close the door.

I turn around and face Daniel and Damon; both of them stand there, staring at me. Daniel's hands are in fists; Damon's are at his side.

"None of this is making any sense. This demon is just playing games, and we are just going to let him do it? To us? To her? Really?" Daniel states, taking another few steps into the field. I watch him run his hand through his hair. Damon and I watch him start to pace back and forth.

"What would you like us to do, Daniel?" Damon states, coming to my side, us both staring at Daniel pacing.

"I don't know, but we need to do something. All this waiting and sitting around is driving me insane. We should be doing more," Daniel states while he tries to take a deep breath.

"We are doing the best that we can with what we are able to do. Right now the demon is in the blue flames. Let the flames do what they have been created to do," I state, looking over at Damon.

I look at Daniel. He finally stops pacing and sits on the ground. I watch him put his head in his hands.

"Daniel, I know that all of this has been hard on you…on all of us, but we need to trust that it will work out. We can't force it," I state as calmly as I can.

Daniel pulls his head out of his hands and stares and me and Damon.

"We have to protect her," Daniel whispers.

"And we will, together," I state, taking a step toward Daniel.

"Nothing is going to happen to Sky," Damon states, also taking a step toward Daniel.

I watch Daniel shake his head. "I hope you guys are right," he states.

"This is how it has to be, Daniel. I know that it is hard waiting, but this is a process, and we have to be smart about how we do things," I state, taking another small step toward him.

Daniel nods. I stare off into the forest, hoping that Gabriel is not far away, that he really is watching all of us. We need him for this to work.

CHAPTER 18

Let Me Stay with You

Argo

Sky stands there staring at me, waiting for me to give her the information she wants. The information I told her I would give her if the men left. She stands there only about a foot away from me.

"So are you going to tell me his plan, Argo?" Sky whispers, searching my face.

The blue flames continue to get hotter; the chains continue to get tighter.

"I will. I keep my word," I state as calmly as I can.

"Since when do demons keep their word?" Sky states.

"I am not like other demons, Sky. Haven't you figured that much out by now?" I ask, amusement in my tone.

I watch Sky turn around and make her way back to the wooden bench. She takes a seat, takes a deep breath, and reconnects her eyes with mine, waiting as patiently as she can.

"He wants you, Sky," I state.

I watch her shake her head. "Tell me something I don't know." She takes in another deep breath and releases it.

"Are you sure you are ready to hear it?" I reply, keeping my eyes locked onto hers.

"Let me guess, he wants me to be his queen. He wants me to choose the side of dark to help him rule. He wants to kill my mates. Am I getting close?" she states in an amused voice.

"It goes much deeper than that, Sky. Yes, of course he wants all those things you have stated, and yes, they are a part of his plan. But you are missing one thing—the most important part of his plan," I state in a low whisper.

I know her mates and Michael are still listening—how can they not? I know of their bond and being able to communicate, but having her ask them to leave was so much fun I couldn't pass up the chance to play one more game with them all.

I watch Sky get up from the wooden bench and take a few steps toward the blue flames; she stops about half a foot away from me. She is braver than I gave her credit for.

"What am I missing?" Sky states, staying put, knowing that she steps any closer, her mates and Michael will break down that wooden door to stop her.

I look deep into her eyes and whisper, "He needs an heir." I watch Sky's eyes go wide. She doesn't move away like I thought she would. I can hear the men on the other side of the door arguing about if they should come back into the yard.

"He wants me to give him children?" Sky whispers. Her voice is soft, filled with pain and despair. I take a deep breath. "No, Sky, he does not want your children. He only wants your son." She takes in a deep breath.

"I don't have a son," she states in a stern voice, trying to hide her fear.

"You will soon enough," I state, not hiding my amusement.

"Who...who will be the father," she asks, barely able to get the words out.

"That I do not know. What I do know is, if he can turn you, then it will also turn your son, hence him getting an heir," I state, watching her closely.

The wooden door finally opens. Sky turns and looks at the door and sees her mates, and Michael standing behind them.

Damon walks in first, then Daniel, then Michael, none of them saying a word but slowly making their way to Sky. She stands there frozen. I can see she is trying to process what I just told her, her mates knowing exactly what I just told her. Daniel and Damon both walk up to her at the same time, both standing there, watching her, only inches away.

"Is it true?" Sky asks, tears filling in her eyes. I watch her allow them to fall. Black and white tears start to fall down her face.

"I don't know, Sky," Michael answers, trying to put together the pieces. "Maybe Gabriel will know," Michael states. I can tell he wants to comfort her, but he is staying his distance, away from her mates.

I watch Damon put his hand on her shoulder. "No matter what the truth is, we would never let you go dark," Damon states, trying to calm her emotions.

Sky takes a deep breath. She slowly turns toward me and takes a small step forward. Damon's hand is still on her shoulder, refusing to let her go.

"I don't believe you. You will say anything—anything—to stay alive," Sky whispers.

"You're wrong, Sky," I whisper back.

She takes another small step toward the blue flames.

She stands there and just stares at me. She doesn't believe me, but soon she will see that what I am saying is true—the light is not the only side that has secrets.

I watch all three men take deep breaths, trying to get ready for whatever I am about to do; none of them is ready for this.

All eyes are on me, but I have to take this chance; if I don't, I don't know the next time I will be able to. I know I will pay a heavy price, but I have to risk it. I look into Sky's eyes, filled with sadness, desire, and longing.

I take a deep breath and reach for Sky with my right hand as fast as I possibly can. As soon as I start the motion, the blue flames get hotter, and the chains get tighter, trying to keep me in place, but it is too late; my hand has already wrapped around her neck. I see all three men try and get to her—Damon trying to pull her back—but the blue flames are already consuming her.

Sky begins to scream. The flames go up and completely wrap around her. I close my eyes and allow my past memories to leave me and enter into her. As soon as they start to enter into her mind, her screams get louder and louder. I open my eyes and see all three men trying to get to her. Damon finally releases his hand from her shoulder, his hand burned.

I hear the wooden door open with a crash. Moments later, Sky is being ripped away from my grip.

"No…no…no…let me stay with you, Sky!" I scream.

Sky falls back into Gabriel's arms. He wraps his arms tightly around her. The chains get tighter and tighter with each passing moment; the flames get hotter, changing into a dark-night blue.

I watch Damon and Daniel move to Sky's back side, both putting a hand on her back. She shoves her head into Gabriel's chest. I watch his grip around her get tighter.

CHAPTER 19

What Have You Done?

The pain from the blue flames is still coursing through my veins, hitting my heart. Each time it enters into my heart, I let out a scream, a scream that echoes throughout the yard and into the forest. I feel the wind pick up and the ground beneath my feet starting to shake. With each scream, Gabriel's grip around me gets tighter. I hear him whispering into my ear, but I can't make out what he is saying. Everything hurts, my soul is screaming out, I can feel Damon's soul and Daniel's soul both wrapping around mine, trying to make the pain go away, but it's not working.

I can hear footsteps, but I can't make out who it is, not until he touches my cheek with the back of his hand—Michael; it is Michael. I focus on his touch, the way his skin feels against mine—smooth, cold, but comforting. I take in a few deep breaths, and slowly the blue flames' pain starts to decrease. With each breath I take, it is slowly decreasing and allowing me to breathe normally.

I can still feel Daniel's and Damon's hand on my back. They are actually working together. *Finally*, I think to myself. After several minutes of leaning in Gabriel's arms, I finally hear Argo stop screaming. I gently start lifting my head from Gabriel's chest and pull away enough to look into his eyes; they are filled with concern and worry. Michael drops his hand from my cheek, and instantly the warm sensation disappears and is replaced with the pain from the blue flames.

I lean my forehead against his chest and take some deep breaths.

"Sky," Gabriel whispers.

I make a small noise. His arms squeeze around me one more time. I feel him begin to pull away. As soon as he releases his arms around me, I turn to the first person and shove my head into their chest; their arms go around me, and once again, I am consumed by the warm sensation. I feel them take a deep breath and slowly release it. I take in a deep breath filled with their scent and quickly realize that I am not in Damon's or Daniel's arms. I gently pull back and look at the face of the one that is holding me—it is Michael.

"Are you okay?" he whispers.

I nod, not knowing what is going on or what the hell just happened. I have no clue what is happening in this moment with his touch.

Michael releases his arms around me and gently pulls away and positions his hands on my arms, keeping me at arm's length away. I look around and see Damon, Daniel, and Gabriel all staring at me. I look over at the demon and see that he, too, is staring at me.

"What have you done to me?" I ask the demon.

"I gave you what you were asking for... I have given you the truth and all the answers," Argo states. His voice is tired, low; his energy has been drained by the flames. I look down at Michael's hands that are holding my arms. There is a hot sensation where his skin is touching my own. I gently take a step back, and he releases his hold, and I watch his hands go down to his sides.

I look around and see that still, all the men are staring at me, waiting for me to say something—anything. I shake my head and take a few steps back. All the men take a step forward; as soon as they do, I put my hands up, motioning them to please stop.

"Sky, are you still in pain?" Damon asks with a concerned voice.

I look into his eyes and see that he is in pain also. Both of my mates can feel what I feel, so that means that whatever just happened with the blue flames, they felt every single thing I did.

"Yes, but I will be okay. I just need a minute to breathe," I whisper. All the men nod at the same time, allowing me to take another step back, making more distance between me and them.

I look over to Argo; his eyes watching my every movement. "You transferred part of your past to me...why?" I state, taking a step closer to him. As soon as I do, all four men take a step forward, preparing to pull me away if need be.

"It was the only way I could give you what you have been asking for. I couldn't speak the words, but the prince never said I couldn't show you," Argo states, taking in a deep breath.

I look at Gabriel, Michael, Damon, and Daniel; all their eyes are on me, waiting for me to say something. I can feel Damon and Daniel both wanting to hold me, comfort me, to take away my pain. I look at Michael, and that is when I realize that whenever we touch, I don't get flooded with anything—this is the same thing that happens with my mates.

I take a step closer to Michael. I take another, and another, until I am only a few inches away from him. I watch his breathing and look into his searching eyes. I slowly bring up one of my hands to his face and gently put my hand onto his cheek—no images, only the warm sensation that I felt before. I look deeper into his eyes. I can see that he knows what I am trying to figure out. I can tell by his body language that he feels the same sensation that I do. I slowly pull my hand away.

"Did you feel that?" I ask in a whisper.

He nods.

"Feel what?" Daniel states, taking a step forward.

I don't answer; I just continue to look at Michael and then turn my gaze to Gabriel. He nods his head, as if to answer my question without me having to say it out loud. I take a deep breath.

"Can someone please tell me what the hell is going on?" Daniel yells. We all turn and look at him. No one is ready for this secret to be revealed just yet.

I take a deep breath. "Everything is okay, Daniel. I promise. I know where the pieces are," I state, trying to get my mates off of whatever is going on between me and Michael.

"Where?" Damon asks.

"In three different places around the world. The first piece is on an island off of the coast of Fiji. The second piece is in the deserts of Arizona, and the third and final piece is in Paris," I state as I make my way slowly to the wooden bench to sit down. All the men move and clear my way to get to the bench.

I take a seat and take another deep breath. All the men turn and look at me, including Argo.

CHAPTER 20

The Future Is Uncertain

Damon

Wwe all stand in place watching Sky make her way to the wooden bench, then take a seat. She looks tired, run-down. I wish I could take all her pain away, but I can't, and she won't let me, even if I could. I make my way to the bench and take a seat next to her. Michael, Gabriel, and Daniel surround the bench but still try and give Sky space to breathe.

I have no idea exactly what just took place between Sky and Argo or Sky and Michael. I feel that all of us are holding back secrets, and eventually secrets always come out, even if we don't want them to.

The rain is still coming down, and by the looks of the clouds, it doesn't appear to be stopping anytime soon. Now we know where the pieces are. The next step we need to take is going to get them, but knowing Argo and Barbas, there are going to be many traps set up to stop us from getting them. Figuring out where the pieces where was the first step; we have many more steps to go before this can be finished.

I have a feeling that whatever is happening between Sky and Michael will not only affect them, but it will, in fact, affect all of us. This might change everything even more than it already has.

"Maybe we all need to get some rest," I state.

I watch everyone look at me. "What about him?" Daniel states as he points to the demon.

"You and I can watch him, Daniel," Gabriel states, putting his hands behind his back.

Daniel nods. He appears to be pleased with the results of who will be watching the demon.

"Yes, I think we all need some rest," Sky states, standing up from the bench. I follow her lead and stand up as well. I watch her make her way over to Daniel. She leans in for a quick kiss and then quickly moves on to Gabriel. "Thank you for what you did," Sky whispers to Gabriel.

"It was my pleasure. You are not just important to Barbas, you are important to us all, Sky," Gabriel states.

Sky turns around and faces me and Michael. "I guess us three should go inside and get some rest. It has been a crazy last few days," Sky states, and she starts to make her way up to the cottage.

Michael and I follow her in silence. I want to ask Michael what happened, but I have a feeling that in this moment, he wouldn't tell me, and neither will she. She has hidden whatever is going on in the deepest part of her mind, and it is going to stay there until she is ready for Daniel and me to know what is going on.

Sky gets to the door and puts her hand on the doorknob; she waits for me and Michael to be behind her, and she turns the knob and pushes the door open. The cottage is warm and smells of the fireplace. This place has become our safe haven from the outside world, and this is where the bond between Sky and me finally reached full connection, not on a physical level but on an emotional and psychological level.

Sky walks in and immediately starts heading down the hallway toward her room. Michael walks into the cottage and instead of heading toward the fireplace, he starts following Sky. I walk into the cottage and close the door behind me, and turn and make my way toward the chairs, facing the fireplace.

I want to go stop him, but I decide that if Sky wants to stop him, she can. She is not big on the whole us-protecting-her thing; she likes to make her own choices.

I take a seat on the chair and look into the fire, waiting for my clothes to dry. I take a deep breath and close my eyes. I allow my thoughts to follow Sky. She might not like us to be right there to protect her, but I refuse to leave her completely alone with Michael.

"Damon," Sky states.

"Sky," I whisper back.

"Keep a watch on Argo, okay? I don't want him to have any more chances to play games," Sky whispers and continues to head down the hallway toward her room.

CHAPTER 21

What Is Happening to Us?

Michael

I calmly follow Sky down the narrow hallway. I am surprised when she doesn't tell me to go away; instead, she is quiet and slowly makes her way to her room. When we get to her door, I watch her take a deep breath and put her hand on the doorknob and turn it. The door slowly opens. Sky takes several steps inside. I follow her lead and walk into the door and turn and close the door. When I turn back toward Sky, she is only about an inch away from me.

My heart starts beating really fast. I can tell by her breathing that her heart is beating just as fast as mine is. I watch her take some steps back and turn around. I take a step forward, taking a deep breath. Sky makes her way to her window and looks out; from here she can see the demon in the blue flames and Daniel and Gabriel watching him and talking to each other.

"Sky," I whisper.

"Michael," she whispers back without turning around.

"Will you please look at me?" I state in a gentle voice.

"I can't," she whispers.

I take another few steps forward. I watch her take a deep breath and slowly release it. I take one more step. My chest is now against her back. I lean down by her ear.

"Sky, please look at me." I take a small step back, giving her room to turn around. At first she doesn't move; she continues to look out the window, then slowly she turns around and faces me.

"What is happening to us, Sky?" I whisper, looking into her eyes.

She searches my face and simply states, "I think you already know."

"This is not possible…none of this is possible, Sky," I whisper.

She leans in closer, only inches away from my face. "You out of anybody should know that anything is possible in our world, Michael." She leans back.

"What do we do from here?" I state, closing the remaining space between us.

"I don't know," she whispers. She begins to turn her face away from me, but I reach my hand up to her face and connect with her cheek, keeping her locked in place, keeping her eyes connected to mine.

As soon as my hand touches her cheek, the warm sensation returns. Every second that goes by, it gets hotter and hotter.

She tries to look away again, but I take my other hand and put it on her other cheek. "Why do you shy away from me, Sky?" I whisper.

"You make me nervous," she whispers.

I feel the warm sensation entering into the rest of my body through my fingers, down my hand, and entering into my arm. The longer I stand still, holding her face, the farther the warmth goes.

"What do you want, Michael?" Sky asks me, looking deep into my eyes.

If someone asked me this question a day ago, it would have been different, but in this moment, feeling this, feeling her, the answer is simple—I want her.

I drop my hands from her face, the warm sensation starting to disappear. I put my hands on her hips and pull her as close to me as I can get her. Both our breathing becomes more rapid and unsteady.

I lean in almost where our lips touch, and whisper, "I want you."

I watch he eyes search my face. She brings up one of her hands and rests it on my cheek.

"Will they know?" I whisper.

Sky shakes her head. "I put up the barrier. I don't want them to find out yet."

I lean in and connect our lips. At first the kiss is gentle, sweet, pure, but then it turns rough, longing, passionate, both of our desires for each other screaming out. I bring up one of my hands and put it against the back of her head, pulling her closer; the kiss deepens. Sky lets out a small moan from her throat. My thoughts are going wild. I can barely keep them under control. I drop my hand from the back of her head and wrap my arms around her waist.

Sky leans in more. I slowly start moving backward, making her follow me. She gives into my wishes, allowing me to lead.

I drop my arms from around her and start bringing up my shirt. I pull away for a moment to pull my shirt over my head. I allow it to drop to the floor. Sky brings her hands up to my chest. I shiver under the touch of her hands on my bare chest. I take my hands and put them at the bottom of her shirt and slowly start bringing her shirt up toward her head. She drops her hands from my chest and lifts them up over her head, allowing me to go through with taking off her shirt.

I drop her shirt on the ground, and we both immediately resume connecting our lips, our hands exploring each other. I feel her hands go to my pants and start to unbutton them. I shiver, feeling her skin on my stomach. I follow her lead and bring my hands down to her pants and start to unbutton them, both of us lost in the passionate kiss, the sensation getting hotter with each second that passes.

We both pull away from each other just long enough to pull down our pants and throw them off to the side, our hands now exploring each other bare, exposed. I never thought in my wildest dreams that I would be in this place.

Sky gently begins to pull away and looks into my eyes. "Are you sure you want this, Michael?" Sky whispers, longing in her eyes, desire that I have never seen before.

I nod. "Yes, I want this… I want you…all of you."

She nods and we reconnect the kiss. I slowly and gently guide us to her bed. I pick her up and lay her down without needing to disconnect the kiss. I pull away slightly and lean down to where my lips are by her ear and whisper, "So this is what it's like to be mated to you," I pull back and allow a small smirk to form from my lips. Sky smiles.

I lean back down and connect our kiss; each second it gets deeper, we become more uncontrolled.

A few hours later

We got lost in each other, both freely giving ourselves, exploring. I knew in these hours she gave me herself fully—all of her—and I gladly returned the gesture.

We lay there in Sky's bed; her head is on my chest, my arm around her, our skins bare for the world to see. With her lying here in my arms, naked and asleep, she is the most beautiful creature I have ever seen.

I look down at my arm and see a blue mark that has spread over all of my body. The mark is dark blue with thorns. I look down at Sky and see that her white mark is now outlined with dark blue. I lie on my pillow and realize that by us connecting in this way, we have allowed the soul-bond to completely form; we are now mated.

There are now three of us, mated to Sky.

CHAPTER 22

Now There Are Three

Damon

Sky and Michael have been in her room for hours, and she has put up the barrier, so I can see and feel everything. I remain seated on the chair. Daniel and Gabriel are still outside watching the demon. I am surprised that Daniel has not come in here already.

I finally hear some movement coming from her room. The doors open and then closes. I hear footsteps coming down the hallway. I finally see Sky. Michael has his hands on her shoulder. The first thing I notice is that he has a dark-blue mark with thorns, and then I notice that Sky's white mark has changed to where it is outlined in the dark-blue color. I take a deep breath.

They both make their way to the couch, and both take a seat. Sky is closest to me, and Michael is on her other side. He gently puts his hand on her leg. I feel Sky finally put down the barrier and allow me to enter. I am flooded with her emotions and thoughts.

I take another deep breath and look at both of them. "Then there were three?" I state as calmly as I can.

I look at Sky, and she nods. "I guess there is."

I shake my head and get up from the chair and kneel down next to Sky. I grab one of her hands in mine and lean down and place a single kiss on her hand. I look up and into her eyes. "The soul-bond is not something we can control. If you are meant to have more mates, well, I am not going to argue."

I watch Sky's eyes fill up with tears. She doesn't try to stop them from falling; instead, she allows them to fall freely. Her tears are now black, white, and dark blue.

"I love you, Damon," she whispers and leans in and connects our lips. I return the gesture and deepen the kiss for as long as I can. After a few moments, we both pull away.

"I love you, too, Sky," I whisper back.

I slowly get up and go back to the chair and take a seat. "So what do we do now?" I ask, looking from Sky to Michael.

Michael looks at Sky for a moment and then looks at me and states, "Wait a few more days and make sure that no one is coming for Argo, then we should get going to the pieces. Sky, what do you think?" Michael asks.

I watch her take a deep breath. "I think whatever you guys think is best. A lot has happened."

"That's not like you," I state in a concerned voice.

I watch her shake her head. "I don't know what to do anymore. Maybe we should ask Gabriel."

I sit there for a moment and stand up from the chair. "Okay, I will go see what Daniel and Gabriel think, okay? I'll be right back."

I watch both Michael and Sky nod. "Okay," Sky states.

I walk to the door and turn my head. I take a deep breath and look out the window; it is still raining. I put my hand on the doorknob and turn the knob and push the door open. As soon as the door opens, both Gabriel and Daniel stop talking and turn to look at me.

I take a few steps outside and close the door behind me. I take a deep breath and make my way down to Gabriel and Daniel. If Sky's barrier is down for me, then I know for a fact that it is down for Daniel.

I make my way down to them. The demon is still right where we left him; he has not tried leaving the blue flames. I think what went down between him and Sky took most of his energy.

"Did you guys get some rest?" Gabriel asks.

"No, not really. I think we are all still tired, but I think it will be that way for a while," I state, looking from Gabriel to Daniel. Daniel is quiet; his body language is still, his hands are forming into fists.

"Did you know?" Daniel asks.

"Did I know what?" I ask, looking him in the eyes.

Daniel shakes his head. "Don't play stupid with me!" Daniel yells.

Gabriel takes a step forward and places his hand on Daniel's shoulder. "What are you talking about?"

I look from Daniel to Gabriel, and then take a deep breath. "Sky and Michael," I state.

Gabriel looks at me and then to Daniel. "So it finally happened."

Daniel turns and looks at Gabriel. "You knew?"

Gabriel nods. "Yes, Daniel, I knew. It was always meant to be. As soon as she mated with you and with Damon, she was fated to also mate with Michael. There was always meant to be three."

"Should we wait a few more days and rest and make sure that no one is coming for Argo, and then leave to go find the pieces?" I ask Gabriel.

Gabriel stands there and then looks at the demon. "Yes, that is a good plan, and I will stay here with the demon."

"And do what with him?" Daniel asks.

"I don't know yet," Gabriel states, looking from the demon, back to me.

"Okay, I will go tell Sky and Michael," I state and turn to start heading back up to the cottage.

"Tell them to come out here. We need to talk about a few things before you all leave and go for the pieces," Gabriel states.

I nod and make my way back up to the cottage. I get to the back door and look through the window. Michael is still sitting on the couch, but Sky is now standing in front of the fire, staring into the flames.

I watch Sky turn and look at Michael, then look at me from the window. She already knows that I want her to come out. She starts making her way to the door. Michael gets up from the couch and follows her lead.

This just got a whole lot more complicated.

CHAPTER 23

You Got to Be Kidding Me

Daniel

D amon is at the door. I see him open the door, and Sky walks out into the rain; not far behind her is Michael. As soon as they both walk out, I see the marks. *You got to be kidding me... This is real—there are three of us. Now not only do I have to share her with Damon, but now I also have to share her with Michael.*

I have learned that the only way the mark spreads and the soulbond is completed is by touch, and both of their marks look completed. I shake my head, not wanting to think about him touching her or her touching him in any way, shape, or form.

I watch Sky and Michael make their way down to Gabriel and me. Damon closes the cottage door and is not far behind them. I start to pace back and forth, trying to keep my thoughts and emotions under control. I knew something was off when Sky put up the barrier, and when she lowered it, she felt off; her thoughts were calculated.

Sky makes her way down to us first. She calmly walks up to me and grabs my arm. The look in her eyes is of concern and longing. I do the only thing that my heart will let me—I lean over and connect her lips to mine. She leans in, returning my gesture; her kiss tells me that she loves me and that everything between us is still there.

After a few moments, she pulls away and release her grip from my arm. She slowly makes her way to the bench and takes a seat. I turn slightly and see that she has positioned herself to where she can look at all of us, including the demon. I turn back around and look aa Damon walks by me and heads to one side of Sky, then I look at Michael; he stops for a moment and looks at me, then makes his way to Sky's other side. I take a deep breath and then turn around to face them and Gabriel.

I watch Gabriel take his own breath. "What did you want to talk to us about?" Damon finally asks to break the silence.

"The dagger or light blade, whatever all of you are calling it," Gabriel states as he runs his hands through his hair.

"What about the dagger, Gabriel?" Sky asks, looking at Gabriel. We are all looking at him, waiting for him to tell us more secrets.

"I want to warn you," Gabriel states.

"About?" I ask, already getting annoyed.

"You all have to understand that the dagger has never been broken before and has never been empty of power. When you put the pieces back together, the dagger will crave power—any power. I warn you all that the dagger does not choose sides. It does not care if the power it absorbs is of the light or of the dark. Be prepared for it to try and sway you to give it what it needs," Gabriel speaks slowly, making his point. "We need to be careful and cautious."

"We all need to get some rest. Gabriel, you stay with Argo, and the rest of us will get some rest," Damon states, standing up from the bench.

"Actually I think I need some air. I will be in, in a while," I state as I turn and start heading toward the wooden door. Right before I can put my hand on the doorknob, Sky grabs my other hand. I look at her.

"I will come with you," she states, her eyes still filled with concern and worry. I nod.

I put my hand on the doorknob and turn it slowly. The wind pushes the door open for us. I begin taking steps out into the field, Sky holding on tightly. She turns and closes the door behind us. I can hear Damon, Michael, and Gabriel all talking about taking shifts with watching over the demon.

The field is dark; the forest ahead is even darker. Sky doesn't say anything; she just follows my lead, making her way through the field with me and into the forest. As soon as we enter the forest, Sky releases my hand. I watch her slowly; her thoughts are a mess, her emotions scrambled.

I put my hand on her shoulder. "Sky," I state, trying to get her to look at me. She doesn't; she continues to walk. "Sky, please stop and look at me." I watch her take a deep breath, and she comes to a stop.

She turns and lifts her head so her eyes can meet mine. "Then there were three," I state with a smirk. Sky shakes her head and allows for a small laugh to escape her lips.

"Sky, I don't know what to say, about any of this. Right when I think that we have everything figured out, there are more twists and turns and secrets that come out," I state, looking her in the eyes. I can tell she wants to look away but she doesn't.

"Daniel, this is confusing for all of us, and there being a third mate came as a surprise to all of us—me included. I never saw this coming," Sky states tears, forming in her eyes. A single blue tear escapes her eyes and instantly reminds me of exactly what we are both talking about. I lift my hand and gently brush the tear away. I hold her face in my hand. She leans in, allowing for our skins to remain connected.

"I would be lying if I didn't say that I am unsettled with the idea of sharing you with yet again another man, but I also know that this was meant to happen. We and you can't control the soul-bond. I just have to ask…"

"What?" Sky whispers.

"Are you ever going to let me fully touch you the way that you have allowed them to?" I whisper, looking into her eyes.

She allows for the tears to fall from her eyes, her cheeks covered in black, white, and now blue tears.

"I am jealous of them, Sky. I am jealous that you have allowed them to be with you fully," I state as calmly as I can, even though she and I both hear the jealousy in my voice.

Sky nods. "Yes"—in a quiet whisper—"when the time is right," she states.

I nod and take a deep breath. I know that what I am asking of her is not fair, but in hell, we almost connected in the way I know we both are desiring. I also know that I respect her and love her and will wait for when she is ready.

I grab her hand, and she instantly squeezes it. We resume our walk into the woods, going in deeper and deeper. The only sound I can hear is the rain. Sky's thoughts and emotions have settled; now we both are at peace, as much as we can be.

CHAPTER 24

Don't Forget What You Are Fighting For

Gabriel

One day later

We are all supposed to be getting rest; that has not happened. Damon, Michael, and I have been up watching over the demon and waiting for Sky and Daniel to return from the forest.

"You knew this whole time…you knew?" Michael asked.

I nod. "Yes, this entire time. I was hoping you would figure it out when you went searching through the scrolls, but you never did. You do now, though." I watch Damon and Michael shake their heads.

"Any more secrets you want to spill?" Damon asks in an amused but annoyed voice.

I allow for a small smirk to escape my lips. "There are thousands of secrets, none of which I will be telling you."

I can hear footsteps on the other side of the door. Before I can turn around and head toward the door, Michael is already heading toward the door. "Be careful to not play fire with fire, Michael," Damon states in a warning tone.

I watch Michael shake his head and put his hand on the doorknob and turn it. He opens the door, and Daniel and Sky walk into the yard hand in hand. I guess they have also found common ground. I shake my head; mates and soul-bonding can make things very complicated for everyone that is involved.

I look down at their hands. Daniel is squeezing her hand. I think he is trying to reassure her and himself that everything is going to be okay.

"So now that we are all here, Gabriel, is there anything else you wanted to tell us?" Damon asks, looking from me to Sky and Daniel, who are standing off to the side from everyone.

"Yes, the three locations where the pieces are. Keep your eyes open and be cautious. Demons love to set traps, so make sure you all stay together, and most importantly, trust one another," I state, looking at each of them.

I watch them all nod. "I will stay here and continue to guard the demon. Once I can get a fallen that I trust, I will come find you guys," I state, slightly turning and looking at the demon; he is hanging on to every word I am saying.

I turn back around and face Michael. "All of you should go inside and pack and get everything ready. No more rest. You all need to get going," I state.

Michael nods and turns and starts making his way up to the cottage. The rest follow, including Sky, who is the last one to start heading to the cottage.

"Sky, can you stay for a moment? I would like to talk to you." I watch her release her hands from Daniel's and stand still, watching her mates go up to the cottage and file inside. Daniel stops and looks back at Sky. She nods and turns and faces me. I watch him stand there for a few moments and finally decides to go inside and closes the door behind him.

Sky walks over to the bench, looking down at the wet grass. It only takes her a moment to get to the wooden bench. She sits down and takes a deep breath and slowly lifts her head to look at me. I follow her lead and make my way to the wet wooden bench. The rain continues to come down, the air is cold, the wind is starting to pick up.

"I haven't asked you this, Sky, but are you okay?" I ask, searching her face.

She sits there for a moment. "Yes, I think so. I am confused as to why this is all happening," she states.

"Well, the dark has always tried overcoming the light. You know that," I state.

"No, that's not what I mean," she whispers.

"You mean the mates…the soul-bond?" I ask and watch her quickly nod her head.

"I wish there was a simple answer that I could tell you, but there is not. The soul-bond was created at the beginning to ensure that there would be a protector for both the light and the dark, and the female would be the protector of both. Sky, everything needs balance," I state. I watch her listen to every word and process them.

Sky shakes her head. She lets out a small laugh.

"What? What is funny?" I ask, a little confused by her response.

"That doesn't really answer my question, Gabriel," she states, laughing a little more.

"Sorry, Sky, that is the best I can do," I state.

"What did you want to talk to me about?" she asks curiously.

"Make sure you watch over your mates, all three of them. This journey you are about to go on will test you all in ways that fighting demons and going through the levels of hell did not," I calmly say.

"I will do my best, Gabriel. My mates are all alphas," she states.

I nod. "Understood, but, Sky, it is extremely important that you all stay on the same side. Okay? Sky, remember what you are fighting for." My voice is low and cautious.

I watch Sky search my face and look deep into my eyes. I have seen this look between her and her mates; her eyes are those that can see right through you to your soul. I understand very clearly the longer I am around her of why the soul-bond chose her.

"Okay, Gabriel, I understand," Sky states as she stands up. I watch her look at Argo and take a small step toward him. "I will see you soon, demon, you and I have some unfinished business."

I watch the demon's eyes go wide. Whatever she has planned for him, I don't think he will be able to survive it.

85

CHAPTER 25

Entering Back into the Darkness

I slowly make my way up to the cottage. The door is already opened for me by Daniel. I see him standing there, patient, his eyes watching me, waiting for me; all of them are waiting for me. Daniel's, Damon's, and Michael's thoughts and emotions are flowing through me.

I walk into the cottage and see that my mates have already packed everything. "Wasting no time, I see," I state with amusement.

"What did Gabriel want to tell you?" Daniel asks, walking over to the couch.

"He just wanted to remind me of what I am fighting for," I state.

"Sounds like Gabriel," Michael states, leaning against the brick and looking into the fire. So many things are becoming habits for all of us, and looking into the fire is high on that light, that and taking deep breaths.

"So how are we getting to Fiji?" Daniel asks.

I look over at Michael. "Blue beam," he simply states.

I look over at Daniel, and he rolls his eyes. I let out a small giggle. *At least we are not flying or taking a boat*, I think to myself.

"So are you going to tell us where the first piece is?" Daniel asks.

"In a cave."

"Of course it is," Daniel states while shaking his head.

I look over at the door and see our backpacks leaning against it. I take a deep breath and make my way to the door and grab the same bag that has been mine since I started on this long journey.

I hear my mates making their way over to the door as well, each of them grabbing a backpack. I turn around and face them, us all staring at one another.

"So how does this work?" Daniel asks.

I shake my head and giggle again. "Seriously, the hand-holding again?" Daniel states with an annoyed voice.

Michael and Damon both smile.

"Yes, Daniel, we have to hold hands," Michael states, trying not to laugh.

"Don't worry, Daniel, it will only be for a few minutes," Damon states, holding out his hand to Daniel.

I watch Daniel shake his head and reluctantly grabs Damon's hand. Damon grabs Michael's hand, and Michael reaches out to me. I take Michael's hand and reach out to Daniel; he grabs my hand immediately. I look around and see that we are all holding hands.

"Michael, I think we are all as ready as we will be," I state calmly.

Michael nods and closes his eyes. A moment later, a blue beam comes through the ceiling of the cottage and surrounds me and my mates. I look at Daniel; his eyes are slammed shut. I look to Damon, and he is looking at me with a smile on his face. I look at Michael, and his eyes are still closed. After a few seconds, I can feel the blue beam picking us up off of the ground and pulling up through the ceiling on the cottage. I look down and see the ground getting smaller and smaller.

Moments pass and everything becomes a blur. I close my eyes and wait for it to end.

"We are almost there, you guys. Hold on just a little longer," I hear Michael yell.

I squeeze my eyes shut as tightly as I can. I feel Michael and Daniel both hold tightly onto my hand.

I feel us beginning to be lowered down. It's like a bad roller-coaster ride, the ones that you regret getting on. After about a minute or so, I feel the ground underneath my feet. Michael squeezes my hand.

"Okay, guys, you can open your eyes now."

I slowly open my eyes. My mates are looking at me. I start to look around and see that we are in an opening. Daniel and Michael both release my hand. I watch my mates let each other's hands go.

I take a step back and continue to look around. We are in a forest. This forest feels different; it feels old and haunted. I see a small cave in the distance. I look down at my feet and see brown grass. The darkness has spread to this place. I can feel this forest giving in to the darkness, unwilling to fight.

My mates take a few steps toward the cave. "Gabriel warned me that there will be a test, a trap that the demons have set up. We need to be cautious," I whisper.

I take a deep breath and start making my way to the cave, my mates continue making their way. Our eyes are open; nothing is happening. We get to about a foot away from the cave, and flames come up from the ground, filling the entrance of the cave.

I shake my head; it had to be fire. Damon takes a small step forward and tries to walk through the cave, but he can't; the flames are too hot, and not only that, but there is a force field surrounding the entrance of the cave, a force field that we can't see, but I can feel is there. He backs away. Daniel steps forward, and slowly, the flames make a small path leading into the cave.

I take a step forward and grab his arm. "Daniel, you can't," I whisper.

He looks at me and leans down and connects our lips; the kiss was short and sweet. He pulls back his head and whispers "I will be okay."

"Michael…," I state.

Michael takes a step forward, and the flames close, and the path disappears. I watch Michael shake his head. The demons were smart; they have made it to where the cave is protected from light. Only a creator of the dark can enter the cave. I look at Daniel; he is looking at the cave. I can tell by his body language and his thoughts that he is preparing himself to enter the cave. He is the only one of us that can.

"No…no, you are not going in by yourself." I release my hand on his arm and take a step forward toward the flame, but they do not open. "You have to be kidding me!" I yell.

"I will be okay," Daniel whispers. I watch him take another step forward, and the flames move aside once again, creating a small path entering into the cave.

"I love you, Daniel," I whisper. I watch him slightly turn around and mouth that he loves me too. He turns back to the path and takes several steps forward. The flames remain still, allowing him to take a few more steps, and then a few more. He continues to take steps, taking him deeper into the cave and away from me. The flames start closing behind him, the path disappearing.

I take a deep breath and watch my mate disappear into the flames.

CHAPTER 26

One Step in Front of the Other

Daniel

As soon as I start making my way down the path, I can no longer hear Sky's thoughts or feel her emotions. I know that I have once again entered hell. I take a deep breath and continue down the pathway. The flames behind me lighting up the cave jump enough that I can see a few feet in front of me.

The deeper I go into the cave, the more unsettled I become. I can hear a voice in my head quietly saying my name, and I realize very quickly that it is not Sky. No, it's a male's voice, a voice I have heard before, a voice that haunts me. I stop when I hear the voice say my name again.

Daniel, I have been waiting for you, my son. I have been waiting for you to return to me, and now you have, the voice whispers in my head.

Barbas—it can't be.

"I have not come back to you. I have come for the piece. Where is it?" I yell, the cave echoing my words.

I hear a laugh inside my head.

Oh, how wrong you are, my son, the voice states.

"I am not your son. Where is the piece!" I scream again.

It is near…you are almost to it, the voice states.

"Who are you?" I ask.

You know who I am, Daniel. You escaped me once. You will not escape me again, the voice yells in my head.

"Barbas?"

Very good, Daniel, he states.

"How? How is this possible?" I ask, a little afraid of the answer.

The X, it did not just bring out who you really were, but it also connected you to me, Barbas states in an amused voice.

I close my eyes and take a deep breath.

I open my eyes and take some more steps down the pathway, trying my hardest to ignore the voice in my head. Barbas, this whole time, he was connected to me; he knew exactly what we were doing, and still he stayed away and let his own demon suffer.

I shake my head and walk around a corner. The pathway comes to an open room, a dead end of the cave. In the middle of the room, there is a stone, flat on top, and the piece of the dagger lying there; no guards, no more tricks, just there for the taking.

I stop at the opening and stare at the piece. *Go ahead, take it. It's yours, a peace offering*, Barbas states.

"A peace offering?" I ask.

Yes, take it. No demon will stop you. It is yours, Barbas states in an amused voice.

"Why...why would you just give it to me?" I ask in a confused and worried tone.

Because it is yours, and you are mine, Barbas whispers in my head.

"I am nobody's. I don't know what the trick is here, but this is just too easy!" I yell.

Barbas is quiet for a moment. At first I think he has left my mind, but he hasn't; I can hear his breathing. This connection—whatever it is—is different than what I have with Sky.

Just take the piece, Daniel. We will talk again soon, Barbas states.

I take a deep breath and take a few steps into the room. I stand still, waiting to see if it is a trap, but nothing happens. I take a few more steps, and then a few more—nothing happens. I get closer and closer to the piece.

I stand in front of it, looking down; all of this for a piece of a dagger. I shake my head and lift my hand. I slowly reach out for the piece. I look around one last time. I am completely alone, or at least on the outside, I am. I gently pick up the piece of the dagger from the stone. The piece is heavy, gray in color. I feel no power radiating off of it like I did before; it is lifeless in my hands.

I turn around and make my way back down the pathway I came. The cave seems colder, darker than it was before. I pick up the pace. I want to get the hell out of here. After a few minutes, I finally see the light coming off of the flames. I continue down the pathway and see the flames, still consuming the entrance of the cave, burning hotter. I stop a few feet away from the flames and hold tightly onto the piece.

That is when I hear Barbas whisper, "Don't forget, I will be watching you, Daniel."

I shake my head and slowly make my way to the flames. When I get close enough, they part and make a small path for me to walk through. I take the last few steps that are in front of me and finally exit the cave. I take in a deep breath of fresh air; the heaviness I felt in the cave is now gone. As soon as my feet hit the brown grass, Sky runs up to me. I open my arms, and she jumps into them. She shoves her face into the side of my neck. I am flooded once again with her thoughts and emotions, her fear and worry radiating off of her. I wrap my arms around her tightly.

I take some deep breaths. "Are you okay?" Sky mummers from my neck.

"Yes, Sky, I am okay."

I gently release my hold on her, and she cautiously takes a few steps back. Damon comes to one side of her, and Michael on the other, all of them looking at me, searching my face.

I gently hold up the piece of the dagger in my hand. All their eyes go to the piece.

"You did it…you got the piece," Sky whispers.

I nod and allow for a small smile to escape my lips.

CHAPTER 27

What Happened in There?

"A re you okay?" I ask Daniel, looking him up and down. He was gone for a while, but by the way he is standing here in front of us, he doesn't realize how long he has been gone.

"Yes, Sky, I am okay. I got the piece. That is all that matters."

I take a small step forward. "No, that is not all that matters, Daniel. What the hell happened in there? Did they try to stop you from taking the piece?" I ask, taking a step back. I want to give him space to breathe, but every fiber in my being wants to take him back in my arms and never let him go. Out of all of my mates, he is the one I worry about the most. I know he is no longer human, but when I look at Daniel, I still see that kind, gentle, pure human I met on the school campus.

As I look at him now, I can finally see him for who he is now— my mate, my lover, and alpha dark protector, and I know I need to start treating him that way. I have been trying so hard to protect him from me, from this world that I forgot that he is a part of my world, a part of me.

"Nothing tried to stop me. It was sitting on top of a flat stone. I took it and came back out. There is nothing else that happened," Daniel states, looking me in the eyes. I still feel that he is hiding something, something he doesn't want me to know, but for now, I will take what he has given and be grateful that now we have the first piece to the dagger.

"So what now?" I ask, looking from Daniel to Michael. He is standing at my side, our arms and hands almost touching.

"We rest here for the night, and tomorrow we will blue beam again to the second piece," Michael states, taking a step back.

I turn and watch him observe the open space. He makes his way over to a spot by the forest. It is facing the cave but a likable distance away from it. Damon follows after Michael.

I turn back around and look at Daniel. He is staring at me. His breathing is steady; his emotions and thoughts are calm. Daniel takes a few steps toward me and grabs my arm.

"Wish we had the blue beam through this whole journey. It would have made things a lot easier," Daniel states with a smile.

I smile. "Yes, it would have. It would have made things a lot faster, too," I state.

Daniel squeezes my arm. "Let's go into the woods and grab some wood for the fire," he states, releasing my arm. I nod and turn and look at Michael and Damon, who are setting up camp. Who would have thought so many things can fit into four backpacks.

Daniel grabs my hand, and we start heading into the forest on the opposite side of where we are making camp. The sun has gone down, and the stars are shining bright in the sky; there are no clouds, rain, or storms here—not yet anyways.

I let Daniel lead me from the opening into the forest. The forest still feels sick, worn out, unable to fight the darkness coming from that cave. When we enter the forest, there are no sounds, no animals, no life.

Daniel continues to take us deeper into the forest. I can feel his desire for me, his yearning; his thoughts are calm and comforting. The rage that is normally consuming him has, for the time being, seemed to disappear. We continue to walk for a while and finally come to another opening; it is a small field with a pond.

Daniel releases my hand and makes his way over to the pond. He turns around and smiles at me. The way he looks in this light is breathtaking, his firm toned muscles coming through his black tight

V-lined shirt, his black tight pants shaping to his perfect legs. I take a deep breath.

I make my way to him slowly. He stands still, facing me, watching me, waiting for me to finally get to him. I watch his chest, his breathing steady. When I get to about a few inches away from him, I stop. I look at his face, his eyes; they are gorgeous. I reach out and grab the bottom of his shirt. He holds his breath.

I gently start bringing his shirt up. He lifts his hands over his head and allows me to pull the shirt off. I drop it to the ground. Daniel's eyes go from his shirt on the ground, back to me. He takes a small step forward; he reaches out and grabs the bottom of my shirt. He now is not the only one holding in a breath. He gently brings my shirt up. I lift my hands over my head, allowing him to continue bringing my shirt up and over my head. He drops it to the ground. We both release the breath we were holding.

I close the rest of the distance between us, our chests touching, skin on skin; the warm sensation begins to grow the longer we touch. I keep my hands at my sides and look into his eyes. His desire is radiating from him, his thoughts screaming loud in my head.

Daniel leans in and connects our lips. At first the kiss is soft, sweet, gentle. My hands remain at my sides, but his, they start exploring my back. I feel his fingertips going up and down my back, leaving goose bumps behind. I shiver underneath his touch. I feel a smile form across his lips.

I try and pull back, but his hands go quickly to my hips, keeping me in place. Daniel pulls his head back slightly, disconnecting our kiss. He leans down by my ear; his lips whisper, "Give in to me."

He pulls his head back and looks me in the eyes. A smirk begins to form on his lips as his hands go from my hips to the button on my pants. He gently undoes the button, never breaking eye contact. I reach my hands out to him and grab his pants and unbutton them.

"Are you ready for this?" I whisper.

"Are you?" he whispers back.

I nod and wait to see what he will do next, giving him all the control.

His hands are still on my pants. I feel him slowly start to lower them, as he lowers his as well, bringing my pants down to my ankles. He unzips my boots and gently lifts each foot, taking the boot off and the pants with it.

As he begins to stand, I feel his fingertips going up my body.

He is driving me crazy. I watch him stand. He puts his hands on top of mine and guides my hands while bringing his pants down. I lower down with them. He takes his hands from mine to his boots and unzips them, lifting each foot and taking the boots off and his pants with them. He grabs my hands and slowly helps me back up.

I stand there, excited and nervous. I have never seen Daniel so sure, so alpha, before. I have to admit, seeing him like this is very hot. He has a whole new side to him now that he is a protector.

Daniel gently wraps his arms around me and begins to lower me to the ground. His touch is soft, kind, yet demanding and yearning. I can feel my heart racing. My breathing is becoming more heavy and less controlled.

He slowly lowers himself on top of me and leans in and reconnects our lips. He released his hold around me, his hands exploring my body. I close my eyes and allow my mate to take me, us both finally giving in to the passion that has been building, us both finally giving in to wanting to be connected to each other in every way.

A few hours later

I lie there on the ground, next to my mate, my leg over his stomach, his arm wrapped around me, my head resting on his chest.

"Did I hurt you?" I hear Daniel whisper.

I shake my head. "No."

"Are you sure?" Daniel asks.

"Yes, I am sure."

"I never want to hurt you," Daniel whispers. I can hear concern in his voice. I slowly lift my head to meet his eyes.

"I trust you."

He leans over and connects our lips. I lean in, wanting more, wanting more of him.

He pulls back after only a few seconds. "We should get the wood and head back."

I nod. Daniel begins getting up, taking me with him. I am still amazed by his strength.

It only takes a few moments, and we are standing up. Daniel releases his hands from me and bends down and grabs our clothes.

He turns to me, handing me my things. "I love you, Sky."

"I love you, too, Daniel."

CHAPTER 28

It Will Take Time to Get Used To

Michael

Sky and Daniel have been gone for a few hours now, but by her emotions and thoughts, I know that she is safe, and she is okay. I look over at Damon. He is sitting by the fire; he doesn't seem worried about them being gone at all. I make my way over to the fire and take a seat on the opposite side of Damon. He is staring into the fire.

"Are you worried?" Damon asks me, looking from the fire to my eyes.

"A little."

"They will be back soon. Daniel has changed, but Sky is safe with him," Damon states.

"Not about that."

"Then what?" Damon asks, looking from me to the forest.

"That he was the only one that could go into the cave."

Damon looks back at me. "It makes sense. He is a dark protector. The demons are not stupid to let light into their places."

"I guess."

I can hear Sky's thoughts getting louder; they are finally heading back. I can hear movement behind me. I turn around and look out at the forest. At first I don't see anything, then I see Sky and Daniel; they are both carrying wood.

I watch them make their way through the opening, heading toward us. I turn back around and look at Damon; he is looking at Sky and Daniel.

It takes them a few minutes to get to us. They walk past me and lay the wood next to the fire. Sky takes a seat next to Damon, and Daniel takes a seat next to me.

I watch Sky put her hand on Damon's leg, and he returns the favor.

"This all seems too easy," Sky finally states, breaking the silence.

"What do you mean?" Daniel asks.

"I mean after everything we have had to go through—fighting the demons, going to hell and the levels—and now the piece was just in a cave guarded only by flames, this just seems like it's a trap," Sky states. Damon puts his hand on top of hers and squeezes, trying to comfort her.

"Maybe they are running out of tricks," Daniel states.

"That is not how things work. Demons always have tricks and plans," Damon states, looking at Daniel.

"So what do we do then?" Daniel asks.

"We keep going. We go for the next piece. No matter what they are planning, it can't change the fact that we need the pieces before we can go to the waters of Edanya," I state, looking from Daniel to Sky and Damon.

"Michael is right. We need to stay on track. Not everything is going to go the way we want it to, and Barbas and the demons might be changing things up to get us off of our game. We have to remember the end goal. Gabriel warned that we all need to stay together and trust one another," Sky states, looking to Daniel, then to me.

We all sit in silence, looking into the fire. I don't think any of us will get rest tonight. I look at Sky, and then look at Daniel. They are acting the way Sky and I did not that long ago. I am not going to ask, but by Sky's thoughts, she has connected with all three of us completely in every way possible.

This is going to take time to get used to, not only sharing her with two other men but also being okay with her being intimate with all of us.

I look at Sky. She is staring into the flames; her thoughts and emotions are calm. I never thought I could feel the way I do about her. Even though she is mated to three men, she makes us all feel desired, wanted, and loved in her own way. At the end of the day, that is all we can ask for.

CHAPTER 29

I Will Do Whatever It Takes

Damon

Sitting here with Sky, feeling her touch, hearing her thoughts, feeling her emotions, still take my breath away. So much has happened since I went to her on that campus. I remember how I was before—cruel, ruthless, selfish, evil—and now she has transformed me into something that is worth her love. Before, I was not worth her love or kindness, but she gave it to me anyway. She knew who I was, and still eventually, she learned to trust me and allowed me inside her walls.

I look around the fire and see Michael and Daniel. The two could not be more different. Michael has not changed like we did— he kept his wings—but Daniel, he has transformed and changed. He has gone from a helpless human to an alpha dark protector. I have respect for him now and trust that he will do whatever it takes to protect and save Sky, just like I know Michael will. The way he looks at her is pure, good.

Now that she has connected with all of us, the bond feels different—more intense, more alive.

Sky, are you hurt? I ask her in her mind.

She looks over at me.

No... Why?

You seem tense, I state calmly.

Damon, I am okay.

Are you worried about when we get all the pieces and have the dagger back? I ask her, looking her in the eyes.

A little. Once we put the dagger back together, we will have to figure out how to get to Barbas.

I think I have a plan for that.

What plan? she asks, her voice filling my head.

You're not going to like it.

She looks at me and searches my face. I watch her roll her eyes. *Did you just roll your eyes at me?* I ask, allowing a small smile to form on my face.

Yes, because if you're plan involves using me as bait again, I am going to scream.

Well, you are going to scream then, I state, trying not to laugh.

She just stares at me.

"Can you guys stop doing that?" I hear Daniel ask.

Sky and I both look at Daniel.

"Stop what?" I ask.

"The communication thing in the mind. We know that is what you guys are doing," Daniel states, not hiding his irritation.

"Damon was telling me his brilliant plan after we get the dagger pieces together," Sky states in an amused voice.

"And what plan is that?" Michael asks.

"Yeah, Damon, tell him what the plan is," Sky states, trying not to laugh.

I look at Michael and Daniel; they are both waiting for me to tell them my plan. The last time we had a plan with Sky as the bait, it worked but other events followed that was not supposed to happen.

"Come on, Damon, just tell us," Michael states.

"We use Sky as bait again. We go back to the cottage, and we wait for him to come," I state, continuing to look at Michael and Daniel.

"That is actually not a bad plan," Daniel states, looking at Sky. "Are you okay with this, Sky?"

I look at Sky and watch her take a deep breath. "We know the plan will work, so do I really have a choice?" Sky asks, looking at me.

"Of course you have a choice, Sky. What do you want to do?" I ask her.

"It's a good plan. We can do it, but you all have to promise me something," she states, looking from me to Daniel, to Michael.

"What?" Daniel asks.

"Promise me you will not let him take me," Sky states in a whisper.

I wrap my arm around her. I watch Michael and Daniel stand up and slowly walk around the fire, and they both kneel down in front of Sky; each of them puts a hand on her leg.

"We promise. He will not take you. He will not touch you," Michael states in a stern and confident voice.

I watch Daniel and Michael get up from the ground, and they walk back over and take a seat. Sky watches them sit down.

"Sky, nothing is going to happen. You have three of us, three of your mates to watch over you," I state.

Sky looks at me, her eyes connecting with mine. "I trust you... I trust all of you."

For the rest of the night, we sit in silence, staring at the fire. I watch Michael and Daniel watch Sky, both of them keeping their eyes on her. I thought, with her mating with all three of us, that it would make things harder, but it actually did the very opposite; now there are three of us watching over Sky and watching out for one another.

I know that Barbas and the demons are up to something, and I know that they are making this way too easy, but I also know that there have not been protectors for centuries, so maybe—just maybe—they are keeping their distance. I take a deep breath and try and enjoy having Sky next to me, because for tomorrow, we will be heading to the next piece, and anything from now until then can happen.

CHAPTER 30

More Secrets

Daniel

The sun is finally coming up. It is time for the moon to sleep and the sun to rise. That means it is almost time for us to go get the second piece. If it is anything like this one, I will be the only one that will be able to get to the piece. Sky, Michael, and Damon will not like it, and it will make them question what is going on even more than what they already are.

We have all promised to not have any more secrets, but the truth is, I think that we are all keeping secrets, secrets that we keep hidden in the darkest part of ourselves, and I know that Michael knows more than what he has stated. Damon has been quiet about the demons and Barbas. I think deep down inside, he has some idea of what they are planning, but he is afraid to say it out loud. And Sky, the secrets she is hiding, is more about each of us, her mates. I take a deep breath.

I sit here watching Sky from across the fire. She has been staring into the flames for hours, not saying anything, not even in her mind. Her thoughts are calm and her emotions are silent.

Damon has not left her side, and she has not tried to move from him. When I look at her, I remember what we just did not hours ago; she gave herself to me fully, in every way she can. The secret I am keeping from her could change everything; it could change the way she and I are, and I am not ready for that to happen.

I know that Michael and Damon will do anything to protect Sky, so if they knew that I am connected to Barbas in any way, they would not let me be anywhere near Sky, and Michael—or even Gabriel—might be me in the blue flames, and there is no way in hell I am going to let that happen. I don't even fully understand what all of this means, and until I do, I will keep this secret to myself and bring it to my grave if I have to.

CHAPTER 31

It Is About Time

Gabriel

The rain is still coming down; the clouds have not gone away, and the demon has not tried anything yet. I have been waiting for one of my fallen to come and guard this demon so I can go to Sky, Damon, Daniel, and Michael. They must have already gotten the first piece by now and will soon be heading for the second.

I hear thunder and lightning in the distance. I look at the demon and see that he is watching me, watching every single move I make. I stand in front of him. He looks away.

"What are you going to do with me?" the demon asks in a low voice.

"I don't know yet. You don't fear death, and I am not going to let you go, so the only option we have right now is you staying in the blue flame. I don't know how you did what you did with Sky, but it will never happen again," I state.

"She doesn't belong to you or them or Barbas," the demon states, looking back into my eyes.

"And she doesn't belong to you either, demon," I state as my hands form into fists.

"Ahh, and there it is."

"There what is?" I ask.

"Even Angels have a little dark side, a violent side…an aggressive side."

"Demon, you don't know anything about me," I state, taking a step back from the blue flames.

"You and I, Angel, are not that different. The only difference between us is that I know who I am, and you…you run from it."

I turn around and take a deep breath. He is trying to get me to lose control, and no matter what he says, I can't let him. I can't give him what he wants.

I hear the wooden door open. I turn and see Skyler; he is one of the fallen that chose to fight for the light. He is one that I know the demons haven't gotten to yet.

Skyler stands there for a moment, then walks into the yard. I watch him close the door behind him.

"Where have you been?" I ask.

"Since you have been here, Barbas and his demons have taken more fallen. We are getting thinner and thinner every day, Gabriel," Skyler states as he looks at the demon.

"They have been taking the fallen for a while now, and even more since Barbas has taken over as the prince," I state, not knowing what else to say. I look at the demon and can see how pleased he is with this information.

"I need you watch this demon for me," I state to Skyler.

"Okay and…"

"And nothing. I need to go to Sky and help them with the other pieces and going to Edanya," I state, taking a few steps toward the wooden door.

"I will watch him," Skyler states, making his way to the bench and taking a seat.

I turn slightly to Skyler and firmly state, "No matter what this demon says to you, don't let him go. Don't let him escape. You hear me?" I state as firmly as I can.

"Yes, Gabriel, I hear you. I won't let him go or escape," Skyler replies, continuing to look at the demon.

I walk to the wooden door and grab the doorknob and slowly turn it, and push the door open. The field is dark water rising from all the rain that has fallen, the grass drowning in the very thing it needs to survive.

I take a few steps and close the door behind me.

I look out into the field; everything about this place is becoming darker. Mother Earth is not happy, and with every passing minute, she is making it very clear that she is not giving up without a fight.

I close my eyes and call for the blue beam to come; it only takes seconds. I open my eyes and look up at the sky and see the blue beam coming down to me. It gently surrounds me. I kindly order it to take me to Sky, Daniel, Damon, and Michael.

I close my eyes and allow it to lift me up and take me to wherever they are.

CHAPTER 32

Consumed by Sand

The sun has finally come up into the sky. I watch my mates pack up camp. They are not saying much, just trying to stay out of one another's way. I tried to help, but they told me no; so instead of helping, I am just sitting here looking at a fire that is almost out, the flames unable to hang on. I look up at the sky and see a blue beam. I jump up.

"Look...look up there!" I yell to my mates.

All of them stop and look at me. "Look up. It's a blue beam!"

"It must be Gabriel," Michael states.

It only takes a few moments for the blue beam to come down to the ground and just as fast for it to disappear, leaving Gabriel kneeling down on one knee on the ground. I watch him stand up. He doesn't say anything at first, just looks at each of us.

"Well, I can see that you are all getting along just fine. I am surprised actually," Gabriel states.

I watch Daniel calmly walk over to Gabriel and present him with the first piece. Gabriel takes the piece and puts it in his pocket. Daniel steps back.

"You found someone we can trust to watch over the demon?" Michael asks, taking a step toward Gabriel.

"Yes, Skyler came and is watching him. Michael, Barbas and the demons have been taking more fallen. Our lines are getting thinner," Gabriel states.

"What does that mean?" I ask.

Gabriel turns and looks at me. "It means that we have no time to waste. We need to get the other pieces before Barbas gets his hands on all of the fallen."

"Shouldn't we go get the fallen before Barbas can turn them?" I ask in a worried tone.

"Are you ready to go back to hell, Sky?" Gabriel asks, taking a step toward me.

I shake my head. "No… I do not want to go back there."

"That is what I thought you would say. The only way to get to them is to go back to hell, which would stop us from getting the pieces. Do you not see what is going on here?" Gabriel asks.

"He is trying to get us to go to him instead of getting the pieces," Damon states.

Gabriel nods. "Yes, and we are not going to fall into his trap."

"Sky, where is the next piece again?" Daniel asks, taking a step closer to me.

"In Arizona, in the desert," I whisper.

This new information about the fallen has me even more worried. If we don't save them, then Barbas and his men will turn them into demons, and that means when the battle comes, I would have to kill those that once were my brothers and sisters.

I don't like the idea of just leaving them there, but I know that Gabriel is right—Barbas is hoping that we go for them instead of going for the pieces. One of his first mistakes was only allowing Argo to know where they were.

I watch my mates start to pack up the rest of camp. I stand there staring at Gabriel, who is now staring back at me. "Is there any way to turn them back?" I ask.

Gabriel shakes his head. "Once the transformation takes place, Sky, there is no reversing it. I'm sorry, but you have to let them go. You have to let them all go."

Before I can say anything back to Gabriel, my three mates are standing by me.

"Time to grab hands again," Daniel states.

He reaches his hand out to me. I grab it and reach my hand out to Gabriel. He gently grabs my hand and reaches out to Michael. Michael grabs Gabriel's hand and reaches out to Damon. Damon takes Michael's hand and reaches out to Daniel. I watch Daniel slowly grab Damon's hand. I stand there watching all of us hold hands. Gabriel looks up to the sky and closes his eyes. I squeeze my eyes shut and wait for the blue beam to come down; it only takes seconds, and I can feel its energy surrounding us and gently picking us off of the ground. I feel both Daniel and Gabriel both squeeze my hand, trying to reassure me that it will be over soon.

Blue beaming is like riding in an uncontrolled roller coaster but a million times worse. After about ten minutes in the air, I feel the blue beam bringing us slowly down. It takes about two minutes, and my feet land on something soft, something that can hold my weight. I open my eyes and look down and see nothing but sand. I look around the circle at the men, and they are all looking around; we are dead smack in the middle of a sandstorm. We all release one another's hands at the same time. I allow my hands to go down to my sides.

"Now what?" Daniel yells.

"Look for a pond, a black pond!" I yell back.

The sun is already setting on this part of the world; night will be coming soon. We all start walking in the opposite direction, trying to find this dark pond. The sandstorm is picking up as the sun is sinking down, allowing the moon to come to life.

I continue taking steps, trying to see anything, but I can't see more than a foot in front of me at a time. The demon was smart with this location—anyone would get lost. I continue walking and walking and walking. I hear Damon, Daniel, and Michael; their thoughts are loud. They haven't found anything yet; my mates are going to come in my direction and search with me.

I decide to stand still and wait for them to come; it doesn't take them long. Damon comes up on my left side, Daniel on my right, and Michael puts his hands on my shoulders. I take a few breaths and start taking small steps again. I have no idea where Gabriel is; he must have not found anything yet.

The sun finally goes all the way down; everything is black. I take a few more steps and see something in the distance. "Do you see that?" I point in front of me.

"Yeah, I see it!" Daniel replies.

"What is it?"

"I don't know!" Daniel yells.

We start making our way to whatever it is in the distance. I slow down and use caution with each step, remembering Gabriel's words about traps.

Whatever is in the distance is getting closer and closer. With each step I take, my emotions and thoughts are going wild. The cave had flames that only Daniel could enter; I can only imagine what they thought up to protect the black pond.

After a few minutes, we finally get close enough that I can see it is the black pond that is surrounded by grass and rocks. The sandstorm is going around the black pond. It is not covering any of the grass or rocks.

We all continue toward the pond. I stop when I am only about a foot away. Michael releases his grip on my shoulders. Damon and Daniel step into the open space next to the pond; Michael follows. I follow behind him.

I look up and see that the pond is in the eye of a sand twister, the sand leaving the pond untouched. I slowly walk toward the pond and stop on the edge, where the grass ends and the pond begins. I kneel down and look at the water. At the bottom of the pond, I can see something that is silver and sticking out from the mud—that has to be the piece.

Damon, Daniel, and Michael kneel down on the other sides of the pond, looking down into the water.

"I don't see any traps," I whisper.

"There are always traps," I hear Gabriel state behind me. I slightly turn around to look at him. "We just have to find the trap," Gabriel states as he makes his way on the other side of Michael and kneels down.

Without saying another word, I lean over the pond and stick my hand in the water. As soon as the water covers my hand, it begins to burn. I look into the water and see my skin beginning to burn off of my hand. I try and pull my hand out of the pond, but I can't. I scream, but I try and pull my hand out again, but I can. Slowly the burns start to spread, heading up my arm; all I can do is scream, no words.

I feel strong hands grab onto my arms from behind me and rip me away from the pond. I land on my side on the ground. Tears fall from my eyes. I look over my shoulder and see Damon. Michael runs over to the front of me and kneels down on the ground next to me, taking my burnt hand into his. I look down and see the burn; it spread up to my elbow. I try and take some deep breaths, but I can't; all I can do is cry. I feel Damon's arm wrap around my stomach. He pulls me to him, my back against his cheek.

"Sky…Sky," Michael whispers.

I look into Michael's eyes; they are filled with worry and concern. Michael tightly wraps one of his hands over my burnt hand and his other hand around my arm. At first, his touch feels like acid hitting my burnt skin. I squeeze my eyes shut. Damon holds me tighter. About a minute later, the pain starts to decrease. I open my eyes and looks down and see that the burn is slowly disappearing.

I look up at Michael. "How…how are you doing that?" I whisper.

He leans in closer, only an inch away from my face, and whispers, "It's an Angel thing." He closes the remaining inch between our faces and connects our lips. I lean in to his touch, his scent filling me, his soul grabbing onto mine.

"Breathe, Sky, just breathe. It will be over soon," Michael whispers.

I try and do what he asks. I take in some deep breaths and release them as slowly as I can, focusing on my breathing. A few minutes go by, and Michael releases his hold on my hand and arm. I look down, and the burn is gone, and my skin has returned back to normal. I look at Michael, and he lets a small smile form across his lips. I lean in and connect our lips. He leans into my touch. I open my mouth, allowing him to enter; he does without having to think. He tastes so sweet, like apples in the summer. He gently pulls away.

"Thank you," I whisper.

"You're welcome, Sky," Michael states as he slowly stands up.

Damon releases his hold on my stomach and slowly lifts us both up. I lean against him, trying to regain my balance.

"Can someone tell me what the hell that was?" I state, looking to Damon.

"You're going to laugh at the name," Damon states.

I look at him, waiting for him to tell me what the hell just happened to me.

"We call it flesh-eater. It is a clear liquid that we created to kill our enemies slowly. It has no scent, no color. It blends in with anything," Damon states.

I take a step toward him; he gently opens his arms. I walk right into them, shoving my face into his chest. "There was the trap," I state into his chest.

I pull back from Damon after a few moments and look back to the pond. I see Michael kneeling down at the pond, but he is not looking at the pond. I follow his eyes and see Daniel standing by the pond with the piece in his hand.

"What the hell?" I state, looking at Daniel.

"How did you do that?" I hear Damon ask. Damon moves behind me. I can feel his chest against my back. He wraps his arms around my waist and pulls me as close to him as I can get.

Daniel just stands there, holding the piece.

I look over to Gabriel and see him stand up and take a few steps forward.

"It didn't burn you," Gabriel states, looking straight at Daniel.

"No...no, it didn't," Daniel states, looking down at his hands.

Daniel takes a step forward and reaches out his hand toward Gabriel with the piece. Gabriel takes a few more steps forward and grabs the piece from Daniel. I watch him put it into his pocket.

CHAPTER 33

Darkness Can Only Be Touched by Darkness

Daniel

I take a few steps back after Gabriel takes the piece from me. I look over at Sky; she is leaning against Damon's chest, his hands firmly on her shoulders. Michael is standing right beside her. I look back to Gabriel and watch him walk over to Sky, Damon, and Michael, all of them looking at me. I want to tell them, I want to tell them the truth, the secret I have been hiding, but how can I tell them that Barbas told me to grab the piece, that he told me the flesh-eater liquid would not harm me?

I hear Barbas in my head, warning me, threatening me, *Don't tell them anything, Daniel. They would not understand, and they would all turn on you*, Barbas states in my head.

You're wrong. She would never turn on me, I respond back in my head.

Yes, she would, and she will right now if you tell her. They don't need to know. All they need to know is that you got the piece! Barbas yells in my head.

"What do we do now?" I ask Gabriel, his eyes looking me over. He stops at my face, searching for something—anything—to explain how I did it. For my sake, I hope he doesn't figure it out.

I watch him take a deep breath. "Let's get out of here and get some rest," Gabriel states, reaching his hands out, waiting for any of us to take them.

Sky is the first one to move; she grabs Gabriel's hand and grabs Damon's with the other. Damon reaches his hand out to Michael; he grabs it and reaches his hand out to me. I cautiously grab his hand. I look at Gabriel; he reaches his other hand out to me. I slowly take his hand.

"Where are we going?" I ask.

"Anywhere but here, please," Sky replies.

"Somewhere safe," Gabriel states as he closes his eyes. I look up and see the blue beam coming down and quickly surrounding us. The blue beam picks us up front the ground and lifts us into the sky. Everything becomes a blur after that. Several minutes pass, and the blue beam is lowering us to the ground and quickly disappears. I look around and see a cabin and a lake with a dock. We all release our hands.

"Where are we?" Sky asks, taking a few steps toward the cabin.

Gabriel takes a step toward Sky. "We are in a remote location in Maine."

Sky slightly turns around. "Maine?"

Gabriel nods. "It is a safe house that we use. It is off the grid, and not many creatures or humans know about this place. We should be safe here for the night. Tomorrow we can move on to the final location to get the last piece of the dagger."

Gabriel makes his way to the cabin. I watch him open the door and step inside. He leaves the door open for the rest of us to follow.

I watch Sky turn toward the lake; she starts making her way toward the dock.

Michael and Damon start making their way toward the cabin. Damon stops and turns his head and softly states, "Are you coming?"

I shake my head. "No… I am going to go talk to Sky."

I watch Damon take a deep breath, and he continues to make his way toward the cabin, following behind Michael. I look back over at Sky; she is sitting down at the end of the dock.

As I walk toward the dock, I see Sky staring into the water, her legs hanging off of the dock only inches away from the water. She looks like she is deep in thought, but I can hear her, and her thoughts are silent.

I finally get to the dock and start slowly making my way down. "I thought you were going to the cabin," Sky states, still looking at the water.

"I was, but I wanted to spend some time with you alone for a little bit," I state. I get to the edge of the dock and take a seat next to her. She finally looks away from the water and looks over at me.

"Are you going to tell me how you got the piece?" Sky asks, searching my eyes.

"I…I don't know. I just stuck my hand in the pond and got it," I reply back, watching her eyes.

"And the cave?"

"I don't know. I just walked toward the flames, and they separated," I reply, doing my best to keep my thoughts hidden.

I watch Sky, and she is searching my eyes; she is looking for whatever I am hiding, but her body language and thoughts are letting me know she is not finding it.

I watch her lower her head and look down at the water. "Sky," I whisper.

She slowly lifts her head and looks at me. I see pain in her eyes. I see longing and desire; it kills me to have secrets from her, so I do the only thing I can do—like so many times before, I lean in and connect our lips. She doesn't move, so I lean in more. I lift my hand and rest it behind her head.

At first she does nothing, then after a few moments, she leans into my touch, giving in to her longing and desire. After a few minutes of being lost in the passion, she gently pulls away a little. I drop my hand from her head. She leans in and rests her forehead against mine; her breathing is heavy.

"I hate it when you do that," she states, trying to catch her breath.

"What?" I ask, already knowing the answer.

"You know what…" She shakes her head and pulls her forehead from mine. "I don't know what you are hiding, Daniel, but when you are ready, I am here to listen."

"I know, Sky, but I have nothing in this moment to tell you, except that I love you." In this moment, I wanted so badly to tell her what was going on between Barbas and me, but the only thing I could think was how darkness can only be touched by darkness, and I knew that the men would lock me away, and Sky, she would never be able to look at me the same. I am afraid of the darkness that might be inside me, and I am afraid I would lose her, and she is the only thing keeping me alive.

"I love you, too, Daniel. Finding the pieces is going a lot quicker than I thought it would," she states, still looking into my eyes.

"Yes... Yes, it is."

"Just please...," she begins to state but stops and just looks at me.

"Please what?"

She leans in close again, leaving only an inch between our lips. "Just please stay with me...don't go anywhere, okay?"

I pull back just a little to get a better look at her. Her eyes are filling up with tears, and unlike so many times before, this time she doesn't hold them back but allow them to freely fall from her eyes. I gently lift my hand and wipe her tears away with my fingers.

"I am right here, Sky. I promise you, I am not going anywhere. I would never leave you."

I lean in and connect our lips again but only for a few seconds, and I pull back. I look out on the lake and see that the sun is already going down. "I think we should get inside."

Sky nods. I stand up and reach my hands out to her. She gladly takes them. I help her to her feet and wrap my arm around her waist, pulling her as close as she can go.

She allows me to lead. We make our way from the dock. The cabin is only a few feet away. I look up on the porch and see Damon leaning against the rail, waiting for us to come. The door to the cabin is open. Sky and I make it to the stairs, and I drop my arm from her waist, allowing her to go first up the stairs. Damon reaches his hand out, and she takes it; he helps her up the rest of the stairs and guides her into the cabin. I follow behind, closing the door.

CHAPTER 34

You Make Me Better Than I Was

Damon

I gently guide Sky into the cabin. She stops when we get inside, looking at her surroundings. This cabin is different from the cottage she and I created. The living room is filled with books, stacks and stacks of books. The fireplace is stone, very old stone that is as high as the ceiling. The paint of the walls is a dark red; parts of the paint is faded. Off to the left of the living room, there is a small kitchen with the same color red; the stove, microwave, and refrigerator are all the same red as the faded walls. There is a small doorway leading out of the kitchen into a small hallway. There are three doors on both sides of the hallway leading down to the bathroom. The floor all throughout the cabin is the same red as the walls. The ceiling is old wood that appear to have been here since this cabin was built, never needing to be replaced.

Sky takes a few more steps, looking around. Gabriel and Michael are both by the fireplace. Daniel makes his way to the chair. Sky takes a deep breath and looks calmly at everyone.

"I think I am going to go lie down."

She squeezes my hand, letting me know that I can come with her. She looks at me and asks, "Can you please show me where my room is?"

"Of course," I whisper, and I lead her down the hallway and stop at the third door to the left of the bathroom. I push the door open. The walls are the same color red. The bed frame is old and wooden. The room is bare; nothing is on the walls. I take several steps inside, guiding Sky. I hear her close the door behind us. She doesn't turn on the lights. She releases my hand and stand still and watch her walk over to the bed. She bends down and unzips her boots, taking each one off. I then watch her stand up and start to unbutton her pants. I know I should look away, but I don't; my eyes are glued to her.

She slowly lowers her pants and takes each leg out. She drops her pants on top of her boots. She then crawls onto the bed. She lies down on her side, facing me. "Will you stay with me?" she whispers.

I nod and make my way to the bed. I lie beside her, flat on my back. She scoots closer and lays one of her legs across my stomach and wraps one of her arms across my chest and lays her head right underneath my neck. I lie still, allowing her to position herself however she would like.

Once she stops moving, I wrap my arm around her, pulling her even closing to me. I can feel her heart beating with mine, like a dance that is in perfect rhythm. Holding her like this feels like the most natural thing in the world, like we have been doing it for centuries, and now it is just a habit.

Sky takes a few deep breaths and whispers, "I think there is something wrong with Daniel. Something doesn't feel right. He is hiding something from me…from all of us."

I hold her tighter. "I know. I feel it, too." I take a deep breath. "But until we find out what it is, we just have to leave it alone."

"I am trying. I promise, but I feel that he is not telling us everything."

"Sky, Daniel loves you, and when he is ready, you will be the first one he tells, whatever it is," I whisper.

She doesn't respond, but I feel her moving. I release my arm and allow her to move. She leans her face closer to my face. I close the distance quickly and connect our lips. She leans in even more, releasing whatever emotions she is holding back before. She wants a release, and I am willing to play my role.

She gently starts getting on top of me, never disconnecting our lips. A small moan escapes her lips. I lift my hands and position them on her back, exploring whatever I can touch. I pull her down, making her lie completely on top of me, her chest against mine. This time I am the one that allows the moan to escape from deep within my throat, the warm sensation getting hotter the longer we touch, the longer we give in to the desire of each other.

Sky gently pulls her lips away from mine and looks into my eyes. Every time with her feels like the first time.

"What do you want, Damon?" she whispers.

"I want you," I whisper back.

A small smile forms across her swollen lips. "You have me… I am yours."

And with that, I wrap my arms around her, and in a quick swift move, she is now on the bed, and I am on top of her. I lean down and reconnect our lips, and in this moment, everything disappears but her; nothing else matters but this moment of bliss we have created together, our hands exploring each other, giving ourselves to each other completely without second thoughts. It is as natural as breathing, giving into my desire and passion for her, and by her behavior, she feels the same way.

The next few hours, we are both lost in each other, giving in to the passion and desire that we have kept locked away, not caring who hears. During this time, I forget that she is mated to three men; during this time, she is mine and I am hers.

CHAPTER 35

The Last Home Stretch

When I open my eyes, I am lying in the arms of Damon. His back is against the wall, and his arm is stretched over my stomach. Connecting with each of my mates on an intimate level is becoming less awkward. They seem to have come to an understanding of allowing me to show affection to each of them in my own way. When I am with one mate, the other two leave us be.

Even though they have come to this silent agreement, I know it is still hard on each of them. They can't hear one another, but all three of their voices and emotions run through me every second of every day. I lie here in my mate's arms staring at the ceiling. One more piece to go, and then we can finally go to the waters of Edanya. I have hope that all of this is almost over, and we can actually end the reign of darkness once and for all.

I don't know what will happen once this is all over or where we will end up; maybe my mates and I will go back to the cottage in England and settle down. I feel Damon starting to move. All my thoughts and emotions must be waking him up. His arm across my stomach gets a little tighter.

"Not yet," Damon whispers.

"What?"

"Not yet… We should stay here on this bed, in this room, for a little longer," he whispers.

I smile. I take a deep breath. "Everyone is already awake and waiting for us. Michael and Daniel are trying to be patient, but they want us to come out and join them."

Damon shoves his face into my neck and kisses my skin; it is soft and sweet.

He pulls his arm from across me and slowly turns onto his back. I turn and look at him; his eyes are still closed. I lean over and kiss his cheek.

I begin getting up from the bed. Damon grabs my arm, keeping me in place. I turn and look at him, his eyes are staring at me. His grip gets a little tighter. He begins pulling me back down to him and connects our lips. The kiss is rough, passionate, dominant. After a few moments, he releases his grip on my arm and begins making his way to the bottom of the bed. He stands up and walks over to me, reaching his hand out to me. I take it without a second thought.

When my feet hit the ground, he pulls me close to him, where my chest is against his. He brings his hand up and places it against my cheek. "I love you, Sky," he whispers.

"I love you, too."

"Let's go out and see what the guys are doing," he states. He grabs my hand and heads toward the door and opens it and starts leading us down the hallway. There is something about him taking charge that makes me go crazy, but then again, all my mates do this behavior—all alphas.

We make our way down the hallway and enter into the living room. Daniel is sitting on the chair, and Michael and Gabriel are both standing next to the fireplace. All of them stop talking when Damon and I enter into the room. Damon releases his hold on my hand, allowing me to make my way over to Daniel. I lean down and give him a quick kiss and quickly move on to making my way over to Michael. He leans in for me and connects our lips—simple, quick and sweet. I pull back and make eye contact with Gabriel, who is watching my every move.

"Good morning, everyone," I state, disconnecting my eyes from Gabriel and making my way over to the couch. Damon is already sitting down, waiting for me. I take a seat on the couch and automatically put my hand on Damon's leg.

"How long do we have to stay here?" Daniel asks, looking from me to Gabriel.

"Until nightfall. It will be safer."

"Where is the last piece again, Sky?" Gabriel asks, still looking at Daniel.

"It's in a museum in Paris," I state, looking from Gabriel to Damon.

"Why would they hide the piece there?" Daniel asks.

"It is the perfect cover…hide it in plain sight," Damon responds, looking at Daniel.

I turn my attention to Michael, who is staring at me still but hasn't said a word.

"Michael, are you going to tell us now where Edanya is?" Daniel asks.

I watch Michael shake his head. "Not until we have the third and final piece."

"Why is that?" I ask.

"Because it is safer that none of you know until the last minute. We never want Barbas or the demons to find out where it is located," Michael states.

I nod.

"There are different entrances to the waters of Edanya. Different Angels know where certain entrances are, but even if one demon finds out one of the locations, it could be a very bad and dangerous thing," Gabriel states.

"Understood," I state. I look over at each of my mates and watch them nod their heads.

CHAPTER 36

There Are Many Things That You Don't Know

Michael

Standing here, listening to everyone talk about Edanya and when we should leave for the last piece, has me in an unfamiliar panic. The only thing I can think about is protecting Sky, and right now, I don't know if any of us can really protect her from the demons or from Barbas. We all talk about how we won't let nothing happen to her, but right now it is just talk; none of us know what we would do if we came under attack.

I take a deep breath and head toward the door. "Where are you going?" Sky asks in a concerned voice.

"I need some air," I state. I open the door and take a few steps onto the deck and begin to close the door behind me, but before I can, Sky stops the door with her hand and takes a few steps onto the deck. She places her hand on top of mine and closes the door.

She drops her hand from mine and begins walking down the steps. I follow her lead.

"Michael."

"Yes?"

"Are you okay? Your thoughts and emotions are everywhere," Sky states with concern.

I continue following her lead onto the dock. We finally get to the end of the dock, and both sit down and hang our feet over the dock. I can feel her eyes burning into me. I take a deep breath. "I am just worried," I whisper.

"Michael," she whispers as she puts her hand on my leg.

I look into her eyes; they are calm and filled with her own concern and worry.

"There is a lot that you don't know, Sky."

"About what?"

"About me, about the dagger, about Edanya."

She continues to look at me, waiting for me to give her more, and I want to; I really want to, but I can't. It is not my place to state anymore. Gabriel is the one that has to tell her and tell the others.

"Michael," she states, squeezing my leg.

I take my arm and wrap it around her waist and pull her as close to me as I can; she lets me, giving into my need to feel her comfort and warmth.

She leans into me, allowing me to tighten my grip around her. She calmly lays her head on my shoulder. "Sky…"

"Yeah?"

"Is it hard?"

"Is what hard?" she asks in a confused voice.

"Loving all three of us?" I whisper.

Sky takes in a deep breath. "No. I thought it was going to be hard, but with the bond complete, it is actually not hard at all. Is it hard for you?"

"What?"

"Sharing me with the other two."

I now take a deep breath; I should have seen that coming, but hearing her say the words out loud still feels like a punch in the gut. "Sometimes."

"Do you think it gets easier?"

"I don't know. Every moment the bond deepens, our souls are intertwined. I guess in a way, maybe," I state.

"What did you mean earlier that there are things I don't know about you?"

"I just meant that I have done things. I have followed orders... blindly. I have had to make some tough choices," I whisper.

"Me to...until..." She stops and gently lifts her head and looks at me. When our eyes connect, I feel her soul grab onto mine.

"Until what, Sky?"

"Until I found my mates—all three of you. Once the bond took its hold, nothing else mattered. And still to this day, I know in my heart that there is nothing I wouldn't do for the three of you," she states, leaning in closer to me.

I lean down and connect our lips. Her confession scares me, but at the same time, it makes my need and desire for her stronger.

She pulls away. "Michael, we might all have to make tough choices here soon. What matters is that we stay together, all of us."

I nod, agreeing with her and also hoping that I can follow through with what she is asking. When she looks at me, when she touches me, when she gave herself to me, it made me realize how much I want to be the man she wants me to be, and it scares me that I might fail her. I might have to do things that go against what she believes is right.

"I think we should go back in. The sun will be setting soon," I state, lifting us both up to our feet.

I drop my arm from her waist and grab her hand and lead us back to the cabin. I can hear the men talking and trying to figure out a solid plan for whatever is ahead of us. Sky and I start making our way up the stairs. The door opens, and Gabriel is standing there, waiting for us to enter the cabin. I lead us inside and head straight for the couch. Damon is on one side. I guide Sky to the couch, and she takes a seat in the middle, and I take a seat next to her. Once seated, she places a hand on my and Damon's leg. Daniel is sitting in the chair, and Gabriel heads back over to the fireplace.

We are all silent, looking at the fire, watching the flames. We silently wait for the sun to sink down and the moon to rise.

CHAPTER 37

What Does This Mean?

Gabriel

As we all wait in the cabin, I observe how the men look at Sky. The soul-bond is very old magic, magic that has been stated to be unbreakable, magic that can't sway or take sides. When it is completed, the soul literally intertwines together for a forever-lasting bond. The bond deepens with every passing second. With the bond comes powers, powers that I can see, by looking at them, they have not figured out yet. The bond is more than just hearing the thoughts and feeling the feelings; the power is much deeper than that.

We all believed that the soul-bond and protectors were lost forever, and now there are four…four protectors and the strongest soul-bond I have ever seen. What does that mean? I am trying to figure that out.

"Do you think Skyler is doing okay with Argo?" Sky asks, looking at me.

I nod. "I think he is doing just fine. He has been with me for centuries. I trust Skyler with my life."

"Do you think that Barbas has found out where Argo is?" Daniel asks.

"I doubt it. The blue flames protect its own location. Unless they find someone that understands the blue beam's power, they won't be able to find him," I state, looking back into the fire.

We once again fall under silence, none of us knowing what to say as we wait to go after the final piece. I have my thoughts about Daniel, but so far, I don't know what it means yet. He is very guarded, and the only one he lets close is Sky. Being a dark protector gives him abilities to handle the darkness, so him being the only one to have the ability to grab the pieces does not surprise me.

I look out the window behind Daniel and see the sun is finally going down. It won't be long now.

CHAPTER 38

Must Blend In

I look at Gabriel, watching him look out the window. I follow his gaze and see that the sun is going down. Soon the moon will take its place in the sky, and it will be our time to leave the safety of this cabin and go after the final piece of the dagger.

I gently get up from the couch. Both Michael and Damon get up as well, followed by Daniel, all my mates looking at me. I take a deep breath and walk over to Gabriel and reach out my hand. He takes it. I turn to Michael and reach out my hand; he takes it and reaches his hand out to Daniel. Daniel takes a step forward and grabs his hand and then reaches his hand out to Gabriel. Gabriel takes a deep breath and grabs Daniel's hand. I look around and make sure that we all have our hands connected. We all look to Gabriel.

"You guys ready for this?" Gabriel asks.

"Yes, as ready as we will be," I state for all of us. I watch Gabriel look up at the ceiling and close his eyes. I close my eyes, preparing myself for what is about to happen. A few moments later, I can feel the energy surround me and Gabriel's and Michael's hand; both squeeze mine at the same time. I squeeze back, reassuring them that I am okay.

I feel the beam start to lift me off of the ground, and before I can think about the ceiling, I feel fresh cool air on my face. I take in a deep breath and open my eyes; we are already into the sky and moving toward the final pieces of the dagger. I look around and see the world is small from up here. All the darkness is down on earth, and the sky, moon, and stars have not been touched by the dark, at least not yet.

Everything becomes a blur. I close my eyes and wait for it to be over. This trip seems longer than the others. My stomach begins to cramp, warning me that it can't take much more of the beam.

"We are almost there!" I hear Gabriel yell.

My ears begin to ring. Michael tightens his hold on my hand, trying to comfort me, but nothing in this moment is going to make me feel better, nothing but my feet on the safe unmoving ground.

After a few minutes, I finally feel the blue beam lowering us to the ground. I take a deep breath and gently open my eyes. All the men are staring at me, watching me. I can hear my mates in my mind telling me to breathe. I have never gotten motion sickness before, but now I guess my body does not like the blue beam. Just my luck.

My feet gently get placed onto the hard ground. I look down and see broken stone. The blue beam puts us all down on the ground and starts to pull up and disappear into the sky.

"I will never get used to that," I whisper.

"Me neither," Daniel states, looking up at the sky and watching the blue beam disappear.

I look down at the broken stone and see that it once was a street, perfect and beautiful, but now time has taken its beauty away. I continue to look around and see that we are in a very old part of Paris. Over the years, Paris has grown and this part has been forgotten, left to be destroyed by Mother Earth.

I release my hold on Michael's and Damon's hands and take a step forward. The buildings are old, and most of them are falling apart, unable to stay together. I turn around and face the men; they too are looking around.

"Where is the museum?" Daniel asks curiously.

"It has to be close," Michael states, taking a step into the broken street.

I look at Damon, and he too has turned around and is scanning the buildings, trying to figure out which one it is.

I take several steps into the street and look around. I decide to walk down the street to see if I can see the building that Argo put in my head. Daniel is not far behind me. He doesn't say anything, just follows and watches, looking at all of the buildings as we pass them.

We spend the next several minutes walking down the street. I look down each side street as we pass them, trying to see the building in my mind, but so far none of them look like the one Argo showed me. I take a deep breath and stop in the middle of the street. I can hear Daniel walking up behind me. He stops when he gets to my side.

"Sky, is something wrong?" Daniel asks.

"No…maybe… I don't know," I state, looking at Daniel.

He grabs my hand and starts walking again, taking me with him. "We will find the building, Sky, we just have to keep looking," Daniel states with confidence.

I take a deep breath and allow him to lead, looking at each building and side street as we pass them. I look ahead and see that we are coming to a dead end. There is a building that looks like it used to be a hospital; it is dark brown, all the windows are broken, the sign on the building falling down, and missing letters.

We get about ten feet away from the building. Daniel is looking it over. I look to the right side and see there is a side street. I start scanning the street with my eyes, looking at each building.

At the end of one of the side street, I see this tall brick building; the bricks are of different colors—brown, gray, and black. The color of the bricks look faded, no longer bright and in their prime. The more I look at the building, the more I feel this odd powerful pull inside my soul, telling me, pushing me, urging me to go to the building. Without saying anything, I start taking steps toward the side street, pulling Daniel with me.

At first he doesn't move. So I pull a little harder. "Sky…what—" He doesn't finish what he was saying; he just follows my lead without any more questions or comments, holding tighter onto my hand. The buildings on both side of the street are wood and broken; most of the roofs have caved in and have given in to nature, trying to take them over.

I take a deep breath, continuing to make my way to the brick building. The closer I get, the clearer I see that the main door of the brick building is wood and has very old carvings of trees, water, and animals.

I stop when I get about five feet away from the big wooden door. Daniel is standing there with me. He releases my hand and takes a few more steps toward the door. He gently lifts his hands and starts outlining the carvings on the door. I call to Michael and Damon in my head; they both tell me to stay put until they get here. I reassure them that I will, but Daniel has a different plan because he starts pushing the door open. There is no resistance from the door; it opens freely with his touch.

I take a small step forward, reaching out my hand, trying to grab the back of Daniel's shirt, but he is already too far away from me. I stare at him and state, "Daniel, we need to wait for the others."

He doesn't turn around nor does he reply. I try to scream at him in his mind, but once again, there is now a barrier, one that I can't seem to get through. I look down at Daniel's feet and see that one of his feet have already entered into the building.

"Daniel, please wait."

He slightly turns to look at me; he gently whispers. "I will be okay."

My heart sinks as I watch him take several steps into the building. He slightly turns around to look at me and lips he loves me as the door closes.

I allow the tears in my eyes to fall down my face. I take a deep breath. I hear Michael and Damon both screaming in my head to wait, wait for them. I know I should listen, but I can't let Daniel be in there alone. I begin to take a step and reach my hand out to touch the door, and before I can touch the carved wooden door, I feel a hand on my shoulder. I look and it is Gabriel. He calmly pulls me back.

"Can you take me to him?" I whisper, looking at Gabriel and allowing for more tears to fall down my face.

I watch him search my face, then my eyes. He slowly shakes his head. "I have tried to blue beam. The building won't let me in. There is a shield around it that I can't get through."

I take a step back. He allows for his hand to fall from my shoulder. "The blue beam can go to hell, but it can't get through an old building?" I yell.

Gabriel nods.

I take another step back. When I do, my back is against something—soft yet hard. I look up and see Damon. He grabs my arms with his hands, keeping me in place.

"Damon," I whisper, allowing for even more tears to fall down my face. His eyes are filled with worry and concern.

"Sky," he whispers back.

I turn my head back around to look at Gabriel. Michael is now standing right beside him, both of them looking at me. Michael takes a step toward me. I try to back away, but Damon holds me in place. His grip on my arms getting tighter.

"Damon, we have to go to him. He can't do this alone," I whisper back.

"Sky, we can't go in. We have tried—that is what took us so long to get here. We were trying to find another way in. The front door is the only way, and it is being protected," he states, taking a deep breath.

"Yes, it is protected. I got a hell of a shock when I tried to touch the building," Michael states, taking a small step toward me. He watches me as he takes another step. He stops when he is about a foot away from me. I reach out my hand, and he gladly takes it. I pull him the rest of the distance until he is about a few inches away.

"So what do we do?" I ask, looking at Michael.

He takes a deep breath. "All we can do is wait, Sky."

I was afraid he was going to say that. I try to take down the barrier in my mind between Daniel and me, but the barrier doesn't move; it just pushes right back.

Both my mates in this moment allow their souls to grab onto mine, trying their best to soothe me and calm me down. After a while, the tears stop rolling down my face. I stand there feeling Damon's hands on my shoulders and Michael squeezing my hand.

Gabriel is standing not that far away, staring at the door, trying to find a way around the shield. I take a deep breath and do the only thing I can—I stand here and wait for my other mate to come back to me.

CHAPTER 39

What They Don't Know Won't Hurt Them

Daniel

Seeing Sky's face when the door closed broke my heart into pieces, but I had to do this alone. I am the only one that can. *You are learning, Daniel*, I hear Barbas state in my head.

I can feel Sky trying to get through the barrier, but so far, she has not been able to. *She won't be able to break it, Daniel. I have learned since all of you escaped hell*, I can hear the amusement in Barbas's voice as he speaks about Sky.

I look around the room and see broken furniture, glass spread across the floor. I never thought they would choose a plan like this. We need to still blend in, but I thought they would have chosen a place surrounded by people, not a place that looks like it has been abandoned for a while now.

I cautiously start taking steps deeper into the building. Nothing appears to be out of place; everything is old and broken. *Keep going, Daniel*, Barbas whispers in my mind.

I shake my head and continue walking through the different rooms. The paintings that used to be so beautiful are now ripped to pieces and lying on the floors of every room. *You will find what you seek*, Barbas states.

"Why are you doing this to me?" I ask.

Everything will come out soon enough, Barbas states, not hiding his amusement.

"I don't want to play your games anymore!" I yell.

I hear him laugh. *You might not want to, but you already are. Why haven't you told them? Why haven't you told her?*

"Told them what?"

"About me?"

I stop for a moment and think about his question—why? Why haven't I told them? Why haven't I told her?

Daniel, you already know the answer to this question, Barbas states sternly in my head. *There is no reason to hide from the truth.*

I am not hiding, I state and resume walking about the building.

Yes…yes, you are. Just say it.

"I would lose her," I whisper.

Would you? Barbas asks.

I nod. "Yes…yes, I would."

I start making my way up the stairs, trying to focus on what I am looking for. I get to the top of the stairs and look around and see three different rooms. I walk to the middle room and stand in the doorway. More broken pictures and glass spread out along the floor. I look out the window and see that the sun is starting to come up, and the moon and stars have finished their shift of watching over Mother Earth.

I scan the room, trying to spot the piece. I look at the window once more and see a silver thing on the window seal. I take a deep breath and take a step into the room. As soon as my feet go over the threshold of the hallway into the room, I feel a very hot sensation starting to go up my leg. I look down and see flames—red and bright-orange flames coming up my feet, making its way up my legs.

I look back at the silver thing on the windowsill. I take a deep breath and try to take a step, but I am stuck in place, the flames getting hotter and continuing to work its way up my body.

"Give in to it, Daniel. Submit to it."

I scream out in pain, stretching my arms out. The flames continue to work its way up my body. I can feel Sky still beating against the barrier, the barrier not willing to give in to her.

Submit, Daniel! I hear Barbas scream in my head. As I stand here with my arms stretched out, the flames continue to move up my body, the flames getting more intense.

"I'm sorry, Sky," I whisper as I fall to my knees. The flames quickly consume the rest of me. I scream as loud as I can, the pain not letting up.

Say the words, Daniel, Barbas whispers.

I take a deep breath and close my eyes. I scream, "I submit! I submit!"

As soon as the words leave my lips, the flames disappear. I gently lower my arms to my sides. I open my eyes and see the piece has moved from the windowsill to only an inch from me on the ground.

"What did I just do?" I whisper as I lean over. I grab the final dagger piece. I look down at it in my hand; all of this for this one piece.

I will see you soon, Daniel, Barbas whispers. I can feel him leave my head. I slowly get up from the ground, holding the last piece. I turn around and start heading down the stairs toward the carved wooden door.

I stand there looking at the door. *What have I just done?* I ask myself. I shake my head and squeeze the piece. I reach out my hand and gently push the door. It obeys my command, and opens. I stand there looking outside, looking at all of them look at me. I look at Sky; her face is red. I can see dried white, black, and blue tears on her cheeks. Damon is standing behind her, his hands on her shoulders. Michael is standing next to Sky, holding her hand.

Gabriel is standing off to the side, looking at me, searching my face, looking me up and down. I take a deep breath and take a step. As soon as my feet hit the ground outside of the building, Sky's thoughts and emotions take over, flooding in like an angry uncontrolled storm. The door closes behind me. I stand there on the step, looking at them.

Sky takes a deep breath and takes a small step forward. Damon allows his hands to fall from her shoulders. Michael's grip on her hand gets tighter, taking the step with her.

"Daniel, what happened?" Sky asks.

I look at her, seeing the longing in her eyes. I turn to Gabriel and take a step down the stairs. I reach out my hand with the piece and wait for him to take it. He eyes the piece and then looks at me, a million questions in his eyes. He takes a small step toward me and reaches out his hand and cautiously takes the pieces and backs away.

I look back to Sky. Her eyes still deadlocked onto me. "I got the piece. That is all that matters," I state as I make my way down the stairs. I begin walking past all of them, not saying another word. I can feel their eyes following me, watching me walk back down the side street.

They are not ready to hear that I have submitted to darkness or that Barbas got what he wanted or that I have turned into the very thing we all have been trying to destroy.

I continue walking down the street and get to the opening. I close my eyes and release my wings from my back. I can feel their heavy weight stretching out.

I can hear Sky screaming in my head for me to stay—to stay with her—but I can't.

So I do the only thing I can—I allow my wings to take me away, far away.

CHAPTER 40

We Can't Trust Anyone

Michael

I hold Sky's hand tightly as we watch Daniel begin to walk down the street. I can feel Sky starting to panic, not knowing what to do. I can feel she wants to go to him, but I tighten my grip on her hand, keeping her in place. We all watch him go down the street; he spreads his wings and takes off into the sky. I look over at Sky and see a single white, black, and blue tear stream down her face. She turns to me, allowing the tears to fall. I release her hand and slowly bring my hand up to her face and gently wipe away her tears with my fingers; she leans into my touch.

She closes the distance between us, shoving her face into my chest and wrapping her arms around my waist. I wrap my arms around her tightly and close my eyes, calling the blue beam to come. It does. In only moments, the blue beam surrounds us. Her arms get tighter around me. The blue beam lifts us off the ground and blurs us up into the sky.

Sky shoves her face even deeper into my chest. I can feel her tears soaking through my shirt. I lower my head by her ear. "We are almost there," I whisper.

I hold her tightly to me, trying my best to take away her pain, her doubt, her longing to know what just happened. My soul grabs onto hers and holds tightly.

After a few minutes, I feel her starting to calm down just as the blue beam is lowering us down to the ground. When our feet touch the ground, she doesn't release me but just hangs on tighter. The blue beam lifts up and disappears into the sky.

"Sky," I whisper.

She doesn't say anything. I can tell by my shirt that she is still allowing the tears to freely fall from her eyes. "Sky…please look at me," I whisper. I gently release my tight hold on her. She begins to pull back her face from my chest. She pulls away enough that I can now see her face and her sad, confused eyes.

"What just happened?" she whispers.

"I don't know, Sky, but we will find out."

"He…he left…he left me," she whispers.

I take a deep breath. "He will be back. None of us can stay away from you for long."

Sky releases her hold around my waist and takes a step back and starts to look around. She looks back at me. "The cabin?"

"It's the only place that is safe, and I wanted to get you out of there."

"Thank you," she whispers.

"Gabriel and Damon should not be that far behind," I state, trying to put her worries to rest.

"What about Daniel?" she states, looking at me.

"I think he will be along sooner than you think."

"I hope so. I can hear him and feel him, but he is not responding to me," she states, taking a few steps toward the dock.

"Do you want to go down to the dock and wait for the others to show up?" Sky asks.

"Sure."

As soon as the words leave my mouth, Sky grabs my hand, and we start making our way down to the dock. This little place is becoming our place together, a place that has not been touched by the darkness. I want to help her through whatever this is, but honestly I am still trying to process it myself.

We get down to the dock, the wood moving with the waves of the river. The water is calm, clear. We make it to the end of the dock, and I help her take a seat. I sit next her to her and put my hand on her leg.

"I don't know what he was thinking," Sky states, looking out on the river.

"I don't know, Sky, but I do know that he loves you."

She turns and looks at me, her eyes sad by my words. "Are you sure?"

"Aren't you?" I ask back.

I watch her take a breath. "Yes… I know that he loves me… but I also know that he is keeping secrets from me, and now he has a barrier up, so I can only access part of his thoughts and feelings."

"Sky, I don't know what is going on, but one thing I do know is Daniel, Damon, and I would never betray you. When he comes, just ask him," I state, watching her eyes search mine. She looks out at the river and takes a deep breath.

"I love you, Michael," she states, as easy as it is to breathe. She states those three words that have changed everything.

"I love you, too, Sky, and I will keep my promise to you."

"What promise was that?" she states, looking from the river to me.

"I promise I will protect you… I promise that I will never leave you," I state, leaning in closer to her.

She watches my lips and slowly leans in and connects our lips together, fitting together like a perfect puzzle piece.

I gently pull away and look at her. "Trust me."

"I trust you, Michael. I trust all my mates. I am just worried… worried that something is going on with Daniel," she states as she continues to look into my eyes.

"I am worried, too, but all we can do is ask him when he returns."

"If he returns," she states.

"Of course he will. You are his mate, and like I said, none of us can stand being away from you that long. Plus it causes us pain if we are away," I state.

Her eyes get curious by my words. She opens her mouth to say something but changes her mind. "Gabriel told me that the deeper the bond, the more painful it is to be apart."

She nods and looks back at the river. By her thoughts and emotions, my words are helping, but they do not completely take the sting away from what just happened. I just hope that Daniel shows up soon.

CHAPTER 41

So Many Questions and No Answers

Michael does the best he can to comfort me, and share words that he believes will help me through whatever this is, but the only thing I can think is—where is Daniel? We have not been apart like this since Damon, Daniel, and I escaped hell. We have all stayed close to one another, so for him to leave me like he did, I know that something is not right; something is, in fact, wrong.

I watch Michael slightly turn around and look toward the cabin. He looks back at me and allows a smile to form across his lips. He gently leans in and gives me a quick kiss and stands up on the dock. He reaches out his hand and takes mine into his and helps me to my feet. I follow his lead as we make our way down the dock toward the cabin. I focus on the wood dock and all the little cracks and broken pieces.

I look up from the wood at the cabin and see Damon and Gabriel standing by the stairs; both are looking at Michael and me. Damon starts making his way down to us. I stop when he is about a foot away from me. Michael continues walking the rest of the way to the cabin. Damon continues walking toward me. His eyes are filled with desire and passion. When he gets to me, he takes my face into his hands and leans in and connects our lips. The kiss is rough, passionate, hot. He allows for a small moan to escape from the back of his throat. He pulls back and leans down by my ear and whispers softly, "I love you."

He pulls back again and looks me in the eyes. "I love you, too, Damon."

He drops his hands from my cheek and grabs my hand. My mates, lately, have had no issues taking control and taking what they want.

Damon leads us to the cabin. Michael and Gabriel have already gone inside, leaving the door open. "Are you okay, Sky?" Damon asks as we walk up the stairs.

"I am doing better," I state.

We enter into the cabin. Damon releases my hand and shuts the door. I head straight for the couch and sit down. I look over at the chair where Daniel normally sits. It brings a sadness to my heart to see the chair empty. Damon takes a seat next to me and Michael takes a seat on the chair. I look over at the fireplace and see Gabriel.

"What took you two so long to get here?" I ask Gabriel.

"We went looking for Daniel, but his scent went cold. Wherever he went, he doesn't want to be found," Damon states while he puts his arm around me and rests his hand on the side of my leg. I lean into him.

I shake my head, thinking about Daniel and where he could be. "Do you think he went back home?"

I look at Michael. "The cottage?" Michael replies.

I nod.

"I don't know why he would go back there."

"Maybe he wanted answers," Damon states, looking from me to Michael.

"Answers about what?"

"The dagger," Gabriel replies. I look at Gabriel. He is looking at the fire. I watch him take a deep breath.

"Argo was the one that helped Barbas to break it into pieces, and Argo was the one that spread them around the world. Argo knows more than what we think he does," Damon states.

"What don't we know?" I state, looking at Michael.

"About the dagger?" Michael asks.

I nod.

Both Michael and Gabriel take deep breaths. "There are many secrets that have to do with the dagger."

"What secrets?" Damon asks.

"Some secrets are meant to stay secrets," Gabriel bluntly states, looking from Damon to me.

"What secrets?" I ask again.

I watch Gabriel take his hands and run it through his hair. "It has been stated before that the dagger does not take sides. That is not exactly true."

"What do you mean?" Damon asks, trying to hide his irritation.

"I mean that the dagger feeds off of whoever wields it, so if it is light that wields it, light is what it serves. If dark wields it, dark is what it serves," Gabriel states, looking straight at me.

"Why the hell did you not tell us this before?" Damon states.

"Like I said, there are many secrets when it comes to the dagger, secrets that have information that must not get to the wrong side," Gabriel states, taking a step toward Damon and me.

Damon calmly stands up from the couch. I look at Gabriel and then look to my mate. I watch his hands start to form into fists, his thoughts and emotions loud in my head. I lean forward and gently grab his hand. At first he doesn't look at me; he just continues to stare at Gabriel, and then looks at Michael. The room is silent; the only thing I can hear is the fire burning the wood and the men breathing, all taking deep breaths. I begin pulling Damon back down to the couch. He allows me to help him sit back down. He allows me to take control.

"Is there anything else we need to know?" I ask as calmly as I can. Damon puts his hand back on my leg, taking several deeps breaths.

"That is all for now. You will learn more when the time is right," Gabriel states. He calmly begins making his way to the door. I watch him put his hands on the doorknob and stop.

He whispers gently, "Sky, knowledge sometimes is not power but a burden. Just remember, once you know something, you can't unknow it," he states as he turns the doorknob and opens the door. He takes several steps onto the porch and closes the door behind him.

CHAPTER 42

Too Many Secrets Will Tear Us Apart

Damon

Sky and I continue to look at the door. Gabriel left before we could ask any more questions, but he finally revealed a secret about the dagger that we needed to know. We need to know more, but I have a feeling that he is done talking for now. I look over at Michael, and he is looking at Sky, waiting for her to look at him, but her eyes are still locked on the door.

"Sky."

"Yeah," she whispers, looking from the door to me, her eyes filled with confusion and a hint of anger.

"This does not change what we need to do," I state, looking over at Michael.

"This changes some things. We need to be careful. If what Gabriel states is true, the dagger can be the end of everything," Sky states, trying to keep her emotions under control.

"Barbas had the dagger. He had it and tried to destroy it. He doesn't know what we know. This can work in our favor," I state, trying to bring the tension down.

"Daniel knows," Sky whispers.

"What?"

"Daniel knows about the dagger," Sky states, looking at me.

I shake my head and bring my hands up to my head and run my fingers through my hair. I calmly get up from the couch and make my way over to the fireplace. I stare into the fire, taking some deep breaths. "This whole you-can-read-our-thoughts-and-we-can-read-your-thoughts thing can be very dangerous, Sky," I state gently, turning around to face her.

"We can't keep it from him, Damon. He has the right to know just like we do," Sky states, searching my face.

"Sky, we need to be careful until we talk to him. We don't know what the hell is going on with him," I state, running my fingers through my hair again.

"Damon is right, Sky. I don't think Daniel means any harm, but he is processing everything just like we are, and we need to be careful," Michael states, looking from me to Sky.

"Well, it is too late now…because he knows."

"Maybe he doesn't," Michael states.

I watch Sky shake her head. "I know he knows. I can feel it."

"Do you know where he is?" I ask, trying to be sensitive to my mate and still get answers.

"No…he still has the barrier up, but I can feel him, and I can still hear some of his thoughts. I know he can hear me, but he hasn't responded."

I watch Michael stand up and walk over to the couch and sit next to Sky. He places his hand on her leg and gently states, "He will return. He has to."

I watch Sky look at Michael and then turn and look at me. I don't know what to say. Everything is becoming more and more complicated with each passing moment. Nothing is working out the way I thought it would. Everything is becoming blurred and confusing.

"So all we can do is wait for him to show up, and then we will go to the waters of Edanya," Michael states.

Sky nods.

I turn back around and face the fire, doing the best I can to keep my own thoughts under control. I am not good at the waiting game, but I know that we have to do this next step together.

There are so many things we do not know, and Gabriel and Michael are not being that forthcoming with the information. All I know is that if we continue to be in the dark about the dagger and Edanya, the secrets are going to tear us apart.

CHAPTER 43

What Do You Want from Me?

Skyler

Since coming to the cottage, it has not stopped raining. Mother Earth is not happy with what is going on, on earth. She is trying to make a statement that she is not going to allow any of us to control her any longer. The sky is dark; the lightning and thunder are echoing through the forest. I sit here on this wooden bench, watching this demon. He has been watching me ever since I came here, not saying a word, but I can tell by his eyes that he is trying to think of a plan—any plan—to get out of whatever Gabriel is planning to do to him.

"There are so many of us left, you know. Your brothers and sisters are turning, giving in to the darkness, welcoming their new home, their new family," Argo states. I watch a grin form across his lips, the chains digging in deeper into his flesh, the blue flames not allowing the wounds to heal before digging in deeper, making sure that it leaves its mark on his body for him to remember, to remember what happened here.

I take a deep breath and remember what Gabriel told me—to not listen or allow him to get inside my head. One thing I can say for this demon is that he is good with his words.

"There are plenty of us, demon, don't worry about that," I state, staring into his demon eyes. There is nothing behind them—no soul to save, no emotions for him to process; there is just a never-ending dark nothingness.

"Are you sure?"

I nod. "You don't know everything, demon. You have no idea what we can do or how many of us there really is."

"I know that there is less than there was yesterday and less than there was an hour ago."

I gently stand up from the bench and take a small step forward. "Be careful, demon… I have never been good with small talk."

The grin on his face gets bigger. "You already have some dark in you, don't you? The fallen was never meant to serve the light. You were all created to serve the dark."

"You know nothing, nothing at all. You are a slave, demon, a puppet for Barbas to play with, and once he gets what he wants, you will mean nothing to him, nothing but a piece in his game of chess."

I watch the demon try and take a breath; his eyes grow darker, my words stinging more than his own. He is trying to get under my skin, but I can tell that I am the one who is getting under his.

I turn and notice that the wooden door has opened. I stand there wondering when the hell the door opened, and that is when I notice someone standing in the doorway—a man, just staring, watching. I take a step toward the wooden door and take a deep breath.

"Who are you?" I ask.

I watch the man take several steps forward, walking through the doorway and into the yard. I shake my head. "Daniel? What are you doing here?" I state in a worried and confused voice.

At first he doesn't respond. I notice that he is not looking at me. I follow his gaze and slightly turn around and see that he is looking at the demon. I look back at Daniel. "Daniel," I state.

He calmly looks from the demon to me; his eyes look tortured, angry, sad. I look behind him and see that he is alone. "Where is everyone else? Sky, Damon, Gabriel, Michael?"

Again he doesn't answer but takes another step forward. I take a small step back, trying to read his face, but it is blank.

"Welcome back, Daniel," the demon states, not hiding his amusement.

Daniel continues to look at the demon. "What do you want, Daniel?" I ask, trying to get some answers to what the hell is going on.

Daniel calmly looks from the demon to me. "Answers… I need answers."

"Answers to what?"

"That is none of your concern," Daniel states, taking another step toward the blue flames.

"It is. I am to watch him."

Daniel takes another step forward. We are now standing side by side. "I just need to talk to him," Daniel whispers.

"Talk only, nothing else," I state, looking at Daniel.

I watch him nod and take a few more steps toward the demon. "That is far enough."

"You don't want to get too close, Daniel. You never know what I might do," the demon states, letting out a small light laugh.

"You have gotten cocky since the last time I saw you, Argo. You weren't talking like this when Gabriel was around," Daniel states, taking another small step forward.

I look from Daniel to the demon. The demon's hands start to form into fists; the chains get tighter.

"What do you want?" the demon asks.

"I want to know more about the dagger," Daniel states.

"Of course you do."

I watch Daniel take a deep breath and slowly walk over to the wooden bench and takes a seat. He places his hands on his legs and stares at the demon, waiting for him to start talking.

"Tell me something I don't know about the dagger," Daniel states, looking at the demon.

CHAPTER 44

The War Is Not Over

Argo

D aniel stares at me, waiting for me to tell him anything about the dagger. By him being alone, something must have happened, but I doubt he is going to tell me what it is. I take a deep breath.

"There is a lot about the dagger that you don't know."

"Like what?"

"I only know what I have heard over the centuries. Some might just be rumors, some might even be lies. It is hard to know," I state, watching his hands begin to form into fists on his legs. I might not be able to play games with Skyler, but I know for a fact I can play games with Daniel. We played many games, him and I, when he was in hell.

"What have you heard, Argo?" Daniel asks, slowly releasing his hands from fists.

"I have heard that the dagger only truly works for the chosen ones. Many, many wield it and feel pieces of its power, but only the chosen ones can unleash what it is meant to do," I state, looking from Daniel to Skyler.

"Who are the chosen?" Daniel asks.

I look back to Daniel. "I have heard it is the protectors, but like I stated before, I don't know what is true and what is not."

"What is its true power?"

"That I do not know. I do know that the protectors are the most dangerous creatures ever created. That is why they were created to watch over light and over dark, to keep balance and order."

I watch Daniel shake his head and close his eyes, trying to process what I am telling him. I do not know as much as he thinks. I am actually telling the truth that I only know what I have been told or what I have heard over the centuries.

"The only one that knows the most about the dagger is Gabriel. He is the only one that has seen its true power," I state.

Daniel locks eyes with me. He is searching my face, my eyes, trying to figure out if what I am saying is actually true.

I watch Daniel stand up from the bench. He takes a small step forward; his hands form back into fists. I can see the rage radiating off of him. I can see what he is becoming. Barbas's plan is working after all.

"I see you, Daniel. I see the real you. The question is, does she?"

"You don't know what you are talking about," Daniel whispers.

"You know what I state is true. You can't lie to me, young Daniel. Don't forget, I was with you when you transformed. I was with you the whole time."

"I can never forget, even if I wanted to. I remember you... I remember you watching as they tortured me... I remember you watching me suffer and doing nothing to stop it... I remember everything!" Daniel yells.

I can't help but allow a smile to escape my lips. "The war is not over, Daniel. In fact, it is just beginning."

"You will lose...he will lose."

I let a low laugh come out of my mouth. "I don't know if you are trying to convince me or yourself, but we both know that is a lie. We are already winning. Each battle, the light has lost. Each battle, our lines get stronger, and more fall at our feet."

I watch Daniel take a deep breath. "You will lose."

Daniel begins to back away. I watch him turn to Skyler. Skyler stands there, watching the both of us. "Make sure you keep an eye him," Daniel states as he walks past Skyler and toward the wooden door.

"Make sure you keep her close, Daniel."

"I will, don't worry about that," Daniel states as he walks out of the door and into the field.

He has no idea what is about to come—none of them do—and I will get to see it all.

CHAPTER 45

And So It Begins

Barbas

Daniel has no idea just how connected we are. I now know where Argo is; he has no idea what he has done. I sit here in this chair, holding another bottle in my hand, filling up the glass—a habit that has become second nature—looking into the fire, waiting for things to unfold. It is getting closer to the end of my plan, a plan that no one will ever see coming.

Argo has suffered the most from this plan, but they did exactly what I thought they would, and he was able to get to Sky, just like I knew he would. Everything is coming together like a present waiting for me to open.

The more fallen I can get, the better, none of them holding out that long them, giving in to the darkness like they should have at the beginning. They were never meant to serve the light, going against their very nature, serving a side that has always been destined to lose and fall at our feet.

I hear a knock on my door. They don't wait for me to say for them to come in.

My door opens, and one of my men step in, keeping the door open, not coming too close, staying their distance from me. "Yes?" I state, taking a gulp from my glass.

"Have you heard from Argo? The men are asking," Seth states in a calm but nervous voice.

"Not directly, but he is fine. Everything is coming together just the way it should."

"What should I tell the men, my prince?" Seth asks.

I take another gulp from my glass. "Tell the men to get ready. We will be leaving soon."

"Leaving where, my prince?"

"Does it matter?" I ask.

"No...no, it doesn't."

"Well, then go tell them to be ready...all of them."

"Even the fallen?" Seth asks.

"Yes, even the fallen. We need all the men."

"Yes, my prince," Seth replies as he turns and walks back out of the room and closes the door behind him.

I slowly get up from my chair, holding tightly onto the bottle and my now-empty glass.

I make my way over to the window and look out of my kingdom, the kingdom I have always wanted. I take a deep breath.

And so it finally begins.

CHAPTER 46

She Is Mine and I Am Hers

Michael

Sky didn't stay in the cabin for very long; she has made her way out to the dock. She is sitting on the end, with her feet hanging off, almost touching the water. She has been staring at the river for a while now. I can hear she is trying to process through everything that has happened. She is struggling but slowly making progress. Slowly accepting the information she was told by Gabriel.

I stand here on the porch, watching her. Gabriel is sitting on the steps, looking out into the forest. Damon is on the deck, looking out at the river, keeping watch over Sky, doing his best to comfort her from a distance. I take a deep breath and slowly make my way over to Damon. I get about a foot away, and he slightly turns to look at me, then turns back around and resumes looking out at Sky.

I take another step and stand next to him, resting my arms on the railing. "You think she is going to be okay?" I ask Damon.

"Yes, she will be fine, but it will take time," Damon states, looking from Sky to me.

Damon takes a deep breath and calmly states, "It does get easier, you know."

I look at him, not hiding my confusion. "What?"

"Sharing her...loving her...and knowing that she loves all of us. It does get easier," Damon states.

"Is it easy for you?" I ask.

"Sometimes...sometimes it is the hardest thing I have ever had to do, but I have watched her. I have watched her with you and with Daniel, and I have felt how she is with me. I know that her love is true for all of us, and if it is hard for us, then I know it has to be hard on her, even though she will never let us know and see that," Damon states, looking me in the eyes.

"I know, Damon. I know. She is mine, and I am hers."

"She is ours, and we are hers," Damon states, staring into my eyes.

I nod.

Even though I do not like his response, I know that he speaks the truth.

CHAPTER 47

I'm Right Here

Daniel

I finally let down the barrier between Sky and me, allowing her inside my head and me inside of hers. I know where she is, and I am coming for her. The others might not be so inviting when I return, but I don't care; the only person I care about is her.

The sun is setting as I finally fly over the cabin. I see Sky sitting on the end of the dock. She is patiently waiting for me to return; her emotions are everywhere, her trying to make sense of everything, trying to make sense of why I left, why I left her.

I begin starting to lower down to the dock. I turn and see that Damon and Michael are on the porch, watching her, watching me; by their body language and their faces, they are getting ready to come to her aid at a moment's notice.

When my feet land on the dock, the dock moves and creates little waves. I watch as Sky moves back and forth with the dock. She doesn't turn around, but she knows that it is me. I can hear her thoughts screaming at me, cursing me for leaving her. I gently lower my wings, and they enter back into my back.

I take a step toward her, waiting for her to turn around.

"That is far enough," Sky whispers.

I stop, confused by her words, wanting to hold her, wanting to kiss her, wanting her to know that I am sorry, but in this moment, she won't hear any of it; she is hurt. I have hurt my mates.

I take a deep breath. "Where have you been, Daniel?" Sky asks as she slowly gets up and stands. She continues to look out at the lake, refusing to look at me.

"I...I..." I pause and watch her as she slowly and cautiously turns around and faces me. Tears are falling from her eyes. She allows me to feel everything she is feeling. I bring my hand up to my chest. My heart feels as if it is breaking into a million pieces.

She just stands there and stares at me. I take a small step toward her. I watch as her breathing becomes more heavy. I take the last small step. I am only about an inch away from her. I gently take my hand from my chest and bring it up to her face, placing it against her cheek. She brings up her hand and puts it on top of mine. She closes her eyes and allows for more tears to fall.

"Sky, I am so sorry," I whisper.

I watch her close the distance between us, and she connects her lips to mine. The kiss is sweet, passionate, sad. I can feel her need for me. I can feel her desire for me, so I can give in to it. I lean into her touch. I return her sweet gesture.

After a few minutes, she gently pulls away. She searches my face, my eyes. She drops her hand from mine and takes a small step back.

"Are you going to leave again?" Sky asks, continuing to look in my eyes.

I shake my head. "No... I promise I will not leave you again."

She shakes her head.

"What?" I ask.

"Actions speak louder than words, Daniel. You told me before that you would never leave me, and still you left. You chose to leave me...you chose to not tell me anything, and even now you are keeping secrets. You are distant. Even now as you stand here with me, you seem far away," Sky states as she begins to takes steps around me.

I grab her arm. She looks down at my hand and then just into my eyes.

"Sky, please, I am right here," I whisper, my grip on her arm getting a little tighter. I feel the dock rock back and forth. I can hear footsteps behind me, stopping only a few feet away.

Sky looks at my hand on her arm and then looks at me; our eyes connected.

"Are you?" she whispers.

"Yes, Sky. I am right here," I whisper back.

I hear the footsteps come closer behind me. I take a deep breath and release my hold on her arm. I drop my hands to my sides, and Sky begins to walk away. I turn and watch her walk between Damon and Michael. They both look at me and turn around and follow her lead.

Be careful, Daniel, I hear in my head. Barbas has returned.

I am, I state back.

Don't do anything stupid, Barbas states.

I won't.

I begin to follow behind Damon and Michael. Sky continues to head back to the cabin.

Gabriel opens the door to the cabin, and Sky makes her way up the stairs and into the cabin. Damon and Michael follow behind, and me behind them. When I step into the cabin, Sky is taking a seat on the couch, and Damon and Michael sit on both sides of her. I make my way to the chair. Gabriel shuts the door and heads over to the fireplace.

I take a seat on the chair and look into the fire. I can feel all of their eyes on me, waiting for me to say something, anything.

I take a deep breath and look over at Sky, Damon, and Michael. "I am sorry I left," I state.

"You're sorry?" Michael replies.

I nod.

"What is done is done," Damon states, looking from me to Sky.

I look straight at Sky. Her eyes are connected to mine. I watch Damon put his hand on her leg, and then Michael puts his hand on her other leg. I feel my hands starting to form into fists, my own breathing becoming more rapid and uncontrolled.

"I see you guys are closer," I state, not hiding my anger.

"You are the one that left," Sky states, not hiding her sadness from me.

"It will take time," Gabriel states.

I look at Gabriel. "What?"

"For things to go back to normal," he states, looking at all of us.

"Yes, it will," Damon replies.

"So what did you find out, Daniel?" Damon asks me.

I look at Damon and then at Sky. "Nothing too important."

You are becoming a better liar, Barbas states inside my mind.

"Nothing?" Sky asks.

I shake my head.

I watch Sky look at Gabriel. Damon and Michael both squeeze her legs.

I follow her gaze. "So what did I miss?" I ask, looking at Gabriel.

CHAPTER 48

There Are More Secrets to Be Told

Gabriel

There is so much tension in this room it can be cut with a knife. "You didn't miss anything, Daniel. You already know what I told Sky," I state, looking to Sky.

"So can we know about Edanya now?" Sky asks, keeping her eyes on me.

I nod and take a deep breath. "Edanya is a piece off of Eden. What that means is that you cannot take anything out of Edanya. It also means that only creatures of the light can enter."

"Well, that won't be a problem," Damon states.

"Actually it is. Daniel is a dark protector, meaning even though he is not darkness itself, he controls the dark, so he may not enter into Edanya," I state, looking at Daniel. His fists get tighter.

I look back over to Sky. "So that means I can't enter... I am both light and dark."

"Actually you can, Sky. The dagger can only be put back together by you and you alone, because you are both a light and dark protector. You are the watcher over all," I state, watching her take a deep breath.

"There is more?" Sky asks.

I nod. "We can't stay in Edanya long. It is not meant for creatures to stay in. The water that is going to put the dagger back together is special."

"Special how?" Damon asks.

"It is special because it can give eternal life."

"Well, we already have that, don't we?" Sky asks.

I nod again. "Yes, you four...you are protectors. You can't die—that I know of—but demons and Barbas does not. The fallen do not, meaning that they can be killed. The water makes it to where the creature has the ability to not die. It is important that we only put the dagger in the water to repair it. We must not take any water from Edanya."

"Am I a protector?" Michael asks.

I nod. "Yes, but a very rare breed. You are an Angel protector, and I have never seen one until you, Michael."

I watch him nod. He looks into the fire, trying to process what I just said.

"And the hits just keep coming, don't they? Anything else you want to tell us?" Daniel states.

I nod. "One last thing," I state, taking a step toward all of them.

"And what is that?" Daniel asks.

"No matter what happens, stay together. Do not let anything come between you four. You understand me?" I state as sternly as I can.

I watch all of them nod.

I look at Michael and nod. "It is time to tell them."

Michael nods and takes a deep breath.

CHAPTER 49

I Promise

Michael

Sky looks at me, waiting for me to tell her the information she has wanted to know. I squeeze her leg. I look over and see Daniel staring at us, waiting also for me to say where the waters of Edanya is. I take another deep breath.

"There are many different entrances. Each pure Angel was told their own personal entrance to guard and protect with our lives. My entrance…" I stop and continue to look at Daniel; my heart is racing. Sky puts her hand on top of mine and gently tightens it. I look from Daniel to her, her eyes promising me that she is mine. "The entrance is deep within the redwood forest in California."

"California?" Daniel repeats.

I nod but continue to look at Sky. For the first time in a long while, her eyes are not filled with sadness or despair; instead it has been replaced with hope and desire.

"When do we leave?" Sky whispers, looking at me.

"Soon. We will leave when the moon is at his highest. It will be the safest," I state, looking from Sky to Gabriel.

I watch him nod and make his way to the door. He doesn't say anything as he opens the door and walks outside. He closes the door behind him, leaving us to talk among ourselves.

"Is there anything else you want to tell us, Michael? It appears that you are the one that has all the secrets," Daniel states, standing up from the chair and walking over to the fire.

"You are the one to talk about secrets, Daniel. You lied when you say you didn't learn anything. What else are you lying about?" I state, looking at Daniel's back. I watch him take a deep breath.

He doesn't turn around and look at me as he calmly states, "You act as if you are better, but you are not. We are the same, you and I."

"I doubt that, Daniel... I doubt that very much," I state, trying to keep my emotions under check. I can hear Sky pleading with me to stop.

"Can you two please stop," Sky states as she gets up from the couch and starts heading down the hallway to her room. Damon and I both get up as well and turn and watch her leave. I can hear her thoughts loud and clear; she is disappointed in how we are acting and is scared about what is to come, and I don't blame her. I think we are all a little scared about the future and what will happen next.

Daniel looks at me and shakes his head and makes his way to the door. He stops before he opens the door. "Watch what you say, Michael. You don't know everything."

And with that, he opens the door and walks outside, closing the door behind him. Damon and I both stand in the living room, both taking deep breaths.

"Michael, you need to go talk to her. It pains me to say this, but she needs you in this moment, not me, not Daniel. She needs you," Damon states as he walks closer to the fireplace and leans against the bricks, looking into the fire.

I say nothing to Damon. I just take a deep breath and prepare myself, prepare myself to be the one thing Sky needs in this moment.

I slowly make my way down the hallway, stopping at Sky's door. She has left it open, knowing that I was eventually going to make my way down to her.

I stand in the doorway and watch her watch out the window. I watch her breathe. I hear her telling me to come in, inside my mind, but I stay where I am, just watching her. We haven't even entered into the waters of Edanya yet, and so many things have already taken place, things that has changed us all.

"You can come in, Michael," Sky whispers, turning around to face me.

"I know," I whisper.

She takes a step forward, continuing to look into my eyes. "What are you searching for?" I whisper.

"I don't know," she whispers.

I take a step into the door and gently close the door behind me. She watches my every move. I take several steps toward her. I watch as her breathing becomes more rapid.

I take another few steps, closing the distance between us. I bring up my hand and gently rest it against her cheek. She leans into my touch, keeping her eyes connected to mine.

"Promise me one more time," she whispers.

I look deeper into her eyes, seeing longing and desire, and also concern and worry; she is afraid I will leave—she is afraid that we will all leave.

"Oh, Sky," I whisper.

"Please promise me."

I lean in, our lips almost touching. "I promise," I whisper and gently connect her lips with mine. She wraps her arms around my neck, pulling me closer to her, making the kiss deeper.

After the minutes pass, we become more intertwined with each other, just letting go. This is probably not the right time to be giving into our desire for each other, but then again, it seems we both need this; we both need each other, so in this moment, we both just let go and let everything else fade away.

CHAPTER 50

I Need You in This Moment...
No One Else, Only You

I did it again; I gave in to the desire and the passion for one of my mates. We lie here in this bed, in this cabin, about to leave for Edanya, and all I can think about is how I need Michael. I needed this. Every time is like the first time with each of my mates; every time we give in to the passion and desire and allow ourselves to finally let go, I am taken to a different world, a world where it is just them and me together.

"Michael," I whisper.

"Sky."

"Thank you."

Michael turns his head and looks at me, confused. "For what?"

"For you...for this...for being here when I needed you and helping me escape," I whisper, looking into his eyes. They are worried, concerned, but also burning with even more desire, more longing for me.

"You don't have to thank me, Sky."

"Yes, I do, because right now I need you, not Damon, not Daniel, only you," I whisper.

I watch him lean over, almost touching our lips. He whispers, "I love you, Sky."

"I love you, too."

"All of this will be over soon. We are almost done with all of this. We just have to hang on a little longer," he whispers, leaning in and kissing my lips; a quick kiss, but the kiss is gentle, kind. Everything that I love about Michael is wrapped up into this kiss. He gently pulls away and looks back up at the ceiling.

I hear a knock on the door. it is Damon.

Michael looks from the ceiling to me. "It is time."

I take a deep breath, and we both make our way off of the bed. Michael calmly picks up our clothes, handing me mine. As we get dressed, I realize that everything is about to change yet again.

"Damon, we will be out soon!" I yell to Damon through the door.

He doesn't say anything, but I can hear him walking down the hallway into the living room.

I place both my hands on the door and gently lean my forehead against the door. I take a deep breath. I can hear Michael coming up behind me. He wraps his arms around my stomach and rests his head on my shoulder.

"Are you okay?" he asks.

"Yes, just trying to prepare myself."

He squeezes me tightly and gently kisses my cheek. "It will be okay. I got you. I promise."

I nod. He releases his hold on me and takes a step back. I slowly lift my head from the door and put my hand on the doorknob… I take one more deep breath and take a small step back so I can open the door. I turn the doorknob and push the door open and take several steps out of the room. Michael follows my lead, and we head down the hallway to the living room.

I see Gabriel standing at the fireplace. Daniel is sitting in the chair, and Damon is standing on the other side of the fireplace, staring at Gabriel. All of them look at me when I enter into the room. I make my to the couch and take a seat. Michael follows and takes a seat next to me.

"Are we ready for this?" Daniel states, looking to each of us.

"As ready as we are going to be," Damon states.

Michael gets up from the couch and takes my hand, helping me to my feet.

I watch Daniel stand up from the chair, staring down at my and Michael's hand that is still intertwined. I can hear him and feel him; he wants to make things better between us, but right now, I just need time.

"Let me guess...blue beam?" Daniel asks, looking at Gabriel.

Gabriel nods. We all take a step forward, connecting our hands with one another.

I close my eyes and wait for it to come.

CHAPTER 51

Welcome to the Entrance of Edanya

Gabriel

I look at Sky, watching her close her eyes, her waiting for the beam to come. I squeeze her hand, trying to comfort her. I don't know why the blue beam affects her like it does, but then again, there are a lot of things about her that is still a mystery to me. I know a lot about what she is and what she can do, but I know little about who she truly is inside. And recently, she is slowly opening up to me and allowing me to see who she really is. Ever since I pulled her out of the trap Argo set up for her, I can tell she actually trusts me now.

I close my eyes and call the blue beam. It comes in only seconds, wrapping around us, consuming us in its blue color. The beam starts bringing us up off of the ground and soon through the ceiling of the cabin. We start blurring through the sky, heading to the redwoods. It has been centuries since I have visited this entrance to Edanya. We all have our own entrance, and we guard it with our lives.

It will not take us long to get to the redwoods. Everything we all have been through has led to this very moment—us being able to put back together the dagger. Sky squeezes my hand back, a kind gesture. She is trying to comfort me. She is like no one I have ever met, and every time I think I know her, she shows a different side to her. The soul-bond chose well when it picked her. It saw something in her, something that we are all going to need if we want to survive this.

The blue beam begins to lower us to the ground gently. When my feet hit the ground, everyone drops their hands but Sky; she holds onto my hand tightly, not wanting to let go. I open my eyes and look over at her; her eyes are still closed.

"Sky, open your eyes. You are not going to want to miss this," I whisper.

Sky waits a moment and then begins slowly opening up her eyes. Her eyes go wide and she stares at the two statues. I follow her gaze and look upon two Angel marble statues, both having ocean-blue eyes, holding onto a dagger, the same dagger we are fighting to put back together. I look at Sky and watch her take a few deep breaths. She releases my hand and takes a few steps forward, staring into the eyes of one of the Angels. They are positioned on either side of the clear shield protecting the entrance to the waters of Edanya. I can see the shield; it is not completely clear but has different colors running through it—blues, greens, yellows, reds.

"This is the entrance?" Daniel asks, taking a step forward.

"Yes, it is."

"Nothing is guarding it," Daniel states in a confused voice.

"There are plenty things guarding it, young Daniel. One of them is the shield, which stops you from entering."

"And the others?" Sky asks, taking another step forward.

"The Angels…they guard the entrance. No one can enter unless they say so," I state.

"Protect it how?" Daniel asks, looking at me.

"That is the other part of the secret."

"More secrets?" Daniel asks, trying to hide his irritation.

I shake my head. "No…no more secrets."

"Then tell us, how do they protect the entrance?" Daniel asks, turning to face me. I turn and look at him, his eyes filled with anger and confusion.

"They test whoever tries to enter. If you pass, they let you into the waters of Edanya."

"And if you don't?" Daniel asks.

Sky turns and looks at me, waiting for me to answer. I take a deep breath.

"You die," Michael states, walking up beside Sky.

"Haven't we already been tested enough? Haven't we already been through enough?" Daniel asks, his hands turning into fists.

I shake my head. "No…no, you haven't."

Sky looks back to the Angels. I watch her take a deep breath. "What are these tests?"

I take a step forward. "The Angels call them trials. There are three trials, three that you must do with each of your mates." As soon as the words left my mouth, Sky looks at me, very confused and a little worried.

"What are they?" Daniel asks.

"Fire, ice, and thunder. The element will test Sky and one of you together. If your intensions are pure, you will pass."

"And if our intensions are not pure?" Daniel asks.

"You die, just like Michael stated. The trials cannot be lied to or overturned. There is no trick that we can use."

"So what do we do?" Sky asks.

"You all walk forward, standing directly in front of them Angels. They will choose which of your mates will do which trial with you," I state, looking at Michael.

"And then?" Damon asks.

"And then you will be consumed by the element for a period of time until the Angel is satisfied and knows what is true," I state, taking another step forward.

I watch Sky take a deep breath. Daniel backs away from the Angels and turns and starts to walk away. Sky, Michael, Damon, and I turn around and watch him. He runs his hands through his hair.

"If any of you have secrets, this is the time to say it, because the Angels will not care who they punish or who they kill. They only care about protecting the waters of Edanya."

Daniel takes a deep breath and turns around. His eyes are tortured, like he is wrestling with telling us something. By his body language, he is fighting to figure out if he should say it or not.

He turns around and stares at Sky, their eyes connected. "I have been keeping a secret," Daniel whispers.

Damon and Michael take a step toward him, and both state "What secret?"

Daniel continues looking at Sky, not responding to Damon and Michael. I watch him take a step forward.

"What have you been keeping from me?" Sky whispers.

"In order to get the third piece of the dagger, I had to do something."

Sky takes a step forward, her eyes deadlocked onto Daniel. "What did you have to do?" she asks.

Daniel takes another step forward, the distance between them getting smaller and smaller. I look over at Michael and Damon, both of them looking at Daniel, their hands forming into fists, both getting prepared to do whatever they have to, to protect Sky.

"I had to submit," Daniel whispers.

CHAPTER 52

We Will All Be Tested

I am standing here, staring at Daniel, trying to understand and process what he just stated. I shake my head. No, it can't be true. He wouldn't do that; he wouldn't give in. What scares me the most is who did he submit to, and why?

I take a last step forward, making the distance between us about only an inch. "You had to submit to whom?" I whisper, not looking away from his eyes.

I watch him take a deep breath, his eyes telling me that I'm not going to like the answer. "You still have your barrier up. Why?" I ask, not hiding my anger.

"Barbas," Daniel whispers, beginning to look away from me.

I lift my hands and cup his face, making him look at me, making sure he can't turn away. His eyes are teary; his breathing is heavy.

"What about Barbas?" Damon asks. I can hear him taking a step closer to Daniel and me.

Daniel looks at Damon and then looks back at me, my hands still keeping his face in place. He slowly lifts his hands and wraps them around my wrists.

"He is the one I submitted to…he is the one I can hear in my head."

"Daniel, what are you talking about?"

Daniel's eyes go from me to Damon. I gently release his face and allow my hands to fall to my sides.

"The only reason I got the pieces was because Barbas was guiding me, and he let me take them, and the only reason I got the third piece was because I submitted to him. That is what I am talking about. This whole time, Barbas and I have been connected…ever since he put this mark on my chest," Daniel states, lifting up his shirt. I see the black X across his chest. I slowly lift my hands and place my hands on his chest, directly over the X. Daniel's breathing gets more heavy, his eyes coming back to me.

"This whole time, you were lying to me. This whole time you knew that Barbas was letting you get the pieces, and you did it anyways. Why, Daniel? Why would you do that?" I whisper, allowing the tears to escape my eyes. No matter how hard I try, I can no longer keep them at bay. They fall like a rainstorm, not willing to give in.

"I had to…for you," Daniel whispers, taking his hand and wiping away my tears.

I shake my head. "I don't understand."

"All I do is for you, Sky," Daniel whispers.

I watch a single black tear fall down his face.

I shake my head. "Daniel, what have you done?" I whisper.

I take a step back from him, and I continue moving back until I run into one of my mate's chests. My mate places his hands on my shoulders and take a deep breath. I can tell that it is Damon. I look to the side and see Michael standing beside us. On the other side, Gabriel is standing next to Damon, all of us looking at Daniel.

"I'm sorry, Sky," Daniel whispers.

"Is there anything else you want to share before we try to get into Edanya?" Michael asks Daniel, not hiding his anger.

Daniel shakes his head. "No…that is all."

I want to believe him, but his eyes are telling me that there is more, and I hope whatever it is does not get us killed during the trials.

Damon releases his hold on my shoulder and takes a step back, allowing me room to turn around. I look up at the Angels; they are still waiting for us to step forward.

"Sky, you must all step forward…even you, Daniel," Gabriel states.

I hear Daniel taking steps closer; he walks over to Damon's other side, all of us standing side by side.

CHAPTER 53

What Else Is There in the Shadows?

Damon

I stand there next to Sky. Daniel comes to my other side; his breathing is heavy. I look at Sky and watch her watch the Angels. We have been through so much together, but nothing like this. The Angels will decide our fate. Daniel has been keeping a lot from us, but I can understand why he did—he didn't want to lose her, he wanted to be able to protect her and be there for her, but he might have done the one thing he didn't want to do; he might have created such a divide that there might be no turning back from the damage.

Some things can't be forgiven; some things will never be forgotten. He was the pure one, the good one, and now he has submitted to the one person we are trying to destroy. He gave in to the darkness in a way he never should have. He is the dark protector, and now he doesn't just watch over it; now he will have to serve it. Submitting can't be undone. The only way for it to be broken is by the death of the prince.

I don't know what Barbas's plan is, but whatever it is, Daniel just walked right into his hands. Barbas knows everything that we are doing; he knows what we are about to do. I have a very strong feeling that Barbas is far from done when it comes to Daniel. Daniel has been his perfect puppet, and Daniel unknowingly has allowed Barbas to become his master.

I grab Sky's hand, hoping that I can put her emotions and thoughts at ease. She is worried and angry, and she has every right to be, but right now, when we are about to go into these so-called trials, we need to all be one. This is not the time for us to be divided.

Sky squeezes my hand. I know that she can hear my thoughts. We have not seen all of the tricks of Barbas, not yet. Whatever else lies in the shadow, I hope we are alive to fight it. Daniel is not the only one that has kept secrets. The light and the dark have many secrets, many things that we have to earn the right to know.

In time, we will learn more. In time, the shadows will not be able to hide away. In time, the whole world will know of Sky and her power.

"Damon," Sky whispers.

"Yes?"

"I need you to promise me something…something that you might not like…but I need you to keep your word."

I look at Sky, waiting for her to tell me, to tell me what she wants me to promise. I can feel everyone's eyes on us. They to want to know, and for some reason, she has put up the barrier; her thoughts are her own.

"No matter what happens, promise me you will not let Barbas take me. Promise me that you will be the one to end my life if need be."

I stare at her, lost for words, trying to process what she is telling me. I can feel all of the eyes burning through me. I know that Michael and Daniel want to say something, but out of respect for their mate, they are doing their best to stay quiet.

"Sky, I…I—"

Sky squeezes my hand. "Damon, you are the only one I trust to have the willpower to do what I am asking. No matter what, Barbas cannot take me." I watch her take a deep breath, and I take my own.

"I promise," I whisper.

I will do everything in my power to make sure that I never have to keep that promise. She is willing to sacrifice herself, but I am not. She talks about my willpower; I am surprised that she can't see how powerless I really am when it comes to her.

CHAPTER 54

I Am Not Who They Think I Am

Daniel

I stand here staring at the Angels, wondering what the trials will be like, what they will do to us to test us to make sure that our intentions are pure. The only problem is now there is nothing pure about me. The man I was on campus when I met Sky, the man that started out on this journey with her, sadly that man no longer exists. Barbas has taken everything from me. He has changed me into something I don't even recognize in the mirror anymore. Damon and I have switched; he is now the light one, the pure one. I am darkness; it calls to me like a moth to a flame.

For so long, I have fought that calling. I have held out for her. I wanted to be the man she wanted me to be, the man she saw in me, but now when she looks at me, it's different. She doesn't look at me the same. She is afraid of me; she is afraid of what I have done. I try to do the right thing, and at the end, what I thought was right was, in fact, tainted by Barbas. Everything I thought was true was his own words in my mind, and I have fallen for every word.

And now once again, I am going to be tested, tested by beings that have the power to kill me, and all they want is the truth—the truth that I can't admit to, that I, in fact, refuse to even think about. I have hurt all of them too much already. I have already hurt Sky too much. The last thing I want to do is cause her even more pain, but as I stand here looking up at the Angels, I am afraid that I might not have a choice but cause us all more pain. We have fought so hard to get to this point, and now that we are here, we might all get destroyed because I refuse to admit who and what I am.

Because the truth is, I am not who they think I am. The truth is, I am not who she thinks I am.

I look over at Sky. She is no longer staring at the Angels; she is looking at me. The anger I saw in her eyes not minutes ago is now gone and replaced with sadness, hope, and longing. Her soul grabs onto mine, tightly holding on. I hear her words in my head, telling me that she forgives me, telling me that I have not lost her. In this moment, my heart is beating faster than it ever has before. I am lost for words.

I begin slowly making my way to her. She stands there, waiting for me to go to her. I finally stand in front of her, waiting for her to give in to me, waiting for her to embrace me. She leans in and connects our lips. In the kiss, there is forgiveness and desire; everything that I had just told her no longer matters in this moment.

After everything I have done, she is unable to stay away. She refuses to block me out. In fact, she opens herself up to me completely, letting me see her deepest fears and desires. As our lips stay connected, I open my eyes and see that we both are allowing for tears to fall down our faces, our hands staying at our sides.

After a few moments, she gently pulls away. She looks into my eyes as she softly states, "I forgive you...please...please don't leave me again."

"I promise never again," I whisper. I back away and go back to where I was standing before, overwhelmed with her thoughts and emotions, not knowing where hers begins and mine ends.

I look up at the Angels and realize in this moment, I am not afraid, for I know now that I can face anything, as long as she is by my side.

CHAPTER 55

The Time Is Now

Barbas

I hear a knock on the door. I take one last gulp from my glass and calmly put down the empty bottle and glass on the marble table. I turn around and take a deep breath. "Come in."

I watch the door open, and Sayble is standing in the doorway. I watch him put his hands behind his back and take a step into the room. His breathing is calm. From head to toe, he is wearing black leather, the leather we only wear when we are about to go to war.

"The men are ready, my prince. They are waiting for you," Sayble states.

I take a deep breath. The time has finally come. The time is now for us to leave hell and go to the cottage where they have been keeping Argo. My plan is finally coming out, and we are ready to do what needs to be done. One way or another, Sky will be mine.

I start walking toward the door. Sayble takes a step backward and stands off to the side, allowing me to exit my room and step out into the hallway. The hallway is bare; no one or thing is there but Sayble and me.

I take several steps down the hallway and stop and wait for Sayble to come to my side. I hear him close the bedroom door and hear him making his way to me. He stops when he gets to my side.

"Are you ready, my prince?" Sayble asks, looking at me.

"Are you ready?" I reply.

"Yes, my prince… I am ready. The men are ready."

"Good. We all need to be ready for what is about to happen," I state, taking steps down the hallway.

"My prince, the men are outside in the field."

I nod and we make our way down the hallway toward the staircase that leads up to the surface. The last time I was up at the surface, I found Sky. I held her; I almost had her. This time, she will not get away from me; this time, I will make my claim on her.

I have been so lost in my own thoughts that I didn't even realize that we are almost up to the surface. Sayble is right behind me, keeping silent, allowing me to think things through. The only advantage we have is that they don't know yet that we are going to go to the cottage. They don't know we will be waiting for them to return with the dagger and with her.

I take the final steps and enter the surface. The air is cold, fresh; the forest is trying to hang on, Mother Earth wanting us to leave but not daring to try and push us out. She makes her presence known but stays her distance, just enough that I can't take her power away.

I begin making my way down the stairs of the volcano. I look down upon the field and see my men—my demons, my fallen that changed because I demanded it—thousands upon thousands waiting for me, waiting for my given order, and today they will get it from me; today I will allow them to kill anyone and anything that gets in their way. I will allow their true nature to come out with no boundaries.

It only takes Sayble and me a few minutes to get down the stairs, my men standing still, watching my every move, watching as I make my way down the stairs to their home.

I step down the last step and land my feet onto the ground. The grass is dead under my feet, nature refusing to give me anything they offer; it turns their back on me and refuses to do my will.

Sayble stands next to me, his hands behind his back. I look at him. He is confident, strong, willing to do anything and everything I demand him to do. Without question, he will ask my men to do what I ask and will not let them betray me.

Sayble looks at me, waiting for my order. "Tell the men it is time to go into the shadows."

"Where do I tell them to go?" Sayble asks.

"Tell them we are heading to England. We are going to the cottage where they are keeping Argo. We will sit there and wait," I state as I close my eyes and enter into the shadows.

I trust that Sayble will give my order, and soon they will be entering into the shadows, and follow me.

One hour later

I take my time in the shadows, looking at the world from a new set of eyes. I have been in hell for so long, locked away in my room drinking whiskey, that I forgot that there is a whole world out here, a world that soon will be mine for the taking.

I finally shadow into England and begin walking the streets, heading to the tavern. The tavern is empty, as empty as it will ever be. I have called every demon to come to my side and be with me when I face Gabriel, Michael, Damon, Daniel, and Sky. The village is empty. Humans don't know about us or what is going to happen, yet again, Mother Earth has warned them in her own way. They have left, the weather making it too hard for them to stay.

I shake my head and begin making my way to the cottage. The forest here is strong; the roots are deep into the earth, the weather taking over everything, making it hard to withstand.

I finally get to the hilltop overlooking the cottage. Argo and my demons—my army—is hiding in the hillside behind the trees, staying within the shadows. Gabriel only has one man watching over Argo—stupid of him—but then again, Gabriel does everything for a reason; he always has a plan.

I hear footsteps behind me. Sayble takes another step and takes his place at my side. He looks down on the cottage. "What are we waiting for?"

"Waiting for them."

"We have the number. We can kill the fallen and take back Argo."

"I know, but remember, we don't just want him. We want her. We have to wait…be patient," I state, looking down on the blue flames.

"You see those flames down there?"

"Yes, my prince,"

"They are not controlled by me nor can a demon or prince make through them. We need the Angel…we need her."

"Yes, my prince," Sayble states as he begins to turn around.

"Tell the men to stay in the shadows. This will not work if they are seen."

"Yes, my prince," he states and walks back into the woods.

I have not waited this long for my men to destroy it for me; we will wait however long it takes.

CHAPTER 56

Your Time Is Almost Up, My Friend

Argo

The blue flames have not allowed my wounds to heal. The flesh around my neck, wrists, and ankles are raw, bloody, and swollen. I have tried many times to try and get free, but the flames are loyal to its master. It will not bow nor change its course without its master's say.

Skyler watches me, making sure that I am tucked away inside these blue flames, making sure the blue-flame chains are tight.

"You look nervous, my friend," I state, watching Skyler pace back and forth. "Are you worried your master is not coming back?"

Skyler stops in front of me, his hands still behind his back. He does the best he can to control his breath and keep it under control. "I have no master, demon. Unlike you, I am free."

"Are you? Are you really free?" I state, watching his eyes search my face.

I watch him start to pace again, pondering my words in his head. "What would happen if you walked away?"

He stops and looks at me. "I wouldn't."

"What if you did? What would happen?"

He shakes his head. "It is against my orders."

"Like I stated before, are you really free?"

"Compared to you, yes...yes, I am free," Skyler states with a smirk.

"Don't worry, your time will be up very soon. You will see that you are, in fact, on the wrong side, but don't worry."

Skyler stares at me. "I will have mercy on you when my prince comes. You can be transformed, not killed."

"I don't want nothing from you. I do not serve your prince."

"Oh, my friend, but you will," I state, watching his anger start to show on his face.

"Your time will come as well. Whatever Gabriel has planned for you, just know by the end of it, you will wish he had just killed you."

"I thought Angels fight for the light and do no harm."

Now you, my friend, have no idea what Angels can and can't do, but soon you will find out," Skyler states as he walks over to the wooden door and leans his shoulder against it.

We now are both playing head games, and by now, we are both very good at it.

I close my eyes and wait for whatever is to come. I know my prince is coming, but will he be too late? That is the question I do not know the answer to.

CHAPTER 57

The Truth Always Comes Out at the End

Michael

Watching Sky forgive Daniel after everything that he has done to us—to her—gives me hope that no matter what any of us does, she will not let us go. She has gone against everything she has ever stood for and learned to be with us, to love us, to claim us as her own; she even lost her wings to stand up for what she believed was right.

I watch Sky turn away from the Angels and start making her way to a redwood tree. I turn and follow her lead. She stops in front of one of the trees and places both of her hands on the strong trunk. I stop at her side and bring up my hand and place it on her lower back.

Sky slowly looks at me. "This forest is strong. This tree is strong. The darkness has not tainted it yet."

"And it won't. The Angels and Mother Earth protect this forest. They protect the waters of Edanya. The darkness can spread to almost anywhere, but it does not have power in Edanya," I state, watching her eyes watch my lips.

"Not yet," Sky states.

"Sky, listen to me—" I stop when she looks deeper into my eyes.

"Barbas has done things that we never thought was possible, and his need for power, it's beyond anything we have ever seen. We don't know what he can or can't do, Michael," Sky states, dropping her hands from the tree.

"Did you mean what you asked Damon to do?"

She stares at me and takes a deep breath. "Yes… I meant every word. Barbas can't have me or any unborn children I might have in the future. I will not let him use me or my children for his games."

"Sky, it will not come to that."

"It will if we can't get into the waters of Edanya. These trials will either save us or destroy us," Sky states, slowly turning back around and facing Gabriel, Damon, and Daniel.

Gabriel takes a step forward. "It is time. We can't wait any longer. All of you must stand in front of the Angels."

I turn around and stand behind Sky. She is trying her best to keep her breathing steady. She nods at Gabriel and then slightly turns to me. She leans in and kisses me, gentle and quick. She then turns to Damon. Damon closes the distance between them. She then leans in and kisses him, soft and quick. Daniel follows Damon's lead and stands before Sky. She leans in and kisses him, gentle and quick. She pulls back and looks at each of us.

She begins taking steps to the Angels, stopping several feet in front of them. I, Damon, and Daniel follow her. I go to one side of her, Damon on the other, and Daniel next to him, all four of us standing in front of the Angels.

We all take a deep breath at the same time. We all look up at the Angels, waiting for something to happen. At first nothing happens, and then the Angels eyes begin to move.

Sky takes a cautious step forward. I watch the Angels eyes look down on her.

"Sky," they both state. "We have been waiting for you."

"You have?" Sky asks, eyeing both of the Angels.

"Oh yes, my child, we have. There has not been a protector like you in centuries. We have been waiting for you and your mates to find your way here."

We all take a step forward, standing next to Sky, looking up at the Angels, watching them just like they are watching us, their eyes scanning over each of us.

"In order to pass, you all will be tested," one of the Angels state.

"Do not take this lightly. The tests are meant to bring out the truth. If you state the truth, you will live. If you deny the truth, you will die. The bond you all share is special and very strong. Work together and you might survive," the other Angel states.

"We are ready," Sky states.

"We hope that is true," both Angels state together.

"When does it start?" Sky asks.

"Now," both Angels state, their eyes glowing, looking over each of us. I can feel their eyes searching my soul. When I look over at the others, I can tell they feel it, too.

CHAPTER 58

Fire Trial

Damon

We all stand here looking up at the Angels, watching their eyes glow brighter. The Angels' eyes stop on me and Sky. As soon as they look at me, I feel this burning sensation starting down at my feet. I look over at Sky, and I see blue flames coming up from the ground and starting to consume her feet. She looks at me, fear in her eyes. I take a few steps toward her and reach out my hand. She takes it. I look down at my own feet and see the blue flames starting to come up my legs.

The burning, at first, is not too bad, a little uncomfortable, but the longer we stand here, the more intense the sensation becomes. Sky tightens her hold on my hand. I look over at her; she is looking at me, her eyes are filled with pain.

I look at the Angels and see them eyeing Sky and me, watching as the blue flames continue to work its way up our bodies, the flames getting hotter. I can feel my insides starting to boil, the blood in my veins starting to feel like acid.

"What are your intentions?" the Angels asks us.

"To put back the dagger and stop Barbas," Sky screams as the flames continue to work its way up our bodies.

The Angels then look to me. "What are your intentions?"

At first I don't answer, their question not processing in my mind. The only thing I can hear is Sky's screams. I look over at her and see Michael and Daniel standing by her, wanting to help her, but they know they can't. They have to sit back hopelessly and watch her burn.

"We will ask again, what are your intentions?" the Angels both state, looking at me.

I look from Sky to them, looking straight in their eyes. "To be whatever Sky needs."

The flames have made their way up to our chests, slowly increasing in heat. Sky squeezes my hand again. I look at her and see white, blue, and black tears falling from her eyes.

"Do you love her?" one of the Angels ask me as the blue flames start working up my neck.

"Yes!" I scream.

"What would you do for her?" the other Angel asks.

"Anything she asks me to."

"Would you die for her?" they both ask me. I can feel Sky's eyes on me, waiting for me to answer their question.

"Yes."

"Do you love him?" the Angels ask Sky.

"Yes," Sky states as the flames get hotter.

"What would you do for him?" they ask.

"Anything!" she screams, trying to not let the pain consume her.

"Would you die for him like he states he would die for you?" they ask her.

At first Sky is silent. I look at her and watch as the tears roll down her face.

"Yes, I would," she whispers.

I can feel the flames starting up my face. Sky and I both scream at the same time, our blood boiling. I look at the Angels as they both look at Sky and me, both of them searching our faces.

"What will you do with the dagger?" they both ask.

Sky and I both scream the answer at the same time, "Kill Barbas!"

As soon as the words leave our lips, the blue flames start to decrease, the earth sucking them back in. Slowly the flames start going back down our bodies, the hot sensation starting to go away, our blood calming down and trying to return back to its original temperature. Sky squeezes my hand; I return he gesture.

After a few moments, the blue flames are sucked back into the earth. Sky and I both fall to our knees, our hand still tightly holding, refusing to let go of each other. Our breathing is heavy. I look over at Sky. She turns and looks at me. Her tears have stopped; her face is almost dry. I take a deep breath.

I slowly stand up and bring Sky with me. As soon as we are on our feet, she quickly closes the distance and releases my hand. She wraps her arms around my waist and shoves her face into my chest. I wrap my arms around her as tightly as I can and take in deep breaths that are consumed with her scent.

CHAPTER 59

Two More to Go

I shove my face into Damon's chest and hold onto him as tightly as I can. I have never felt pain like I just did with those blue flames. My body felt like it was burning from the inside out. I can feel Damon taking deep breaths, trying to slow down his heart-beat. At the moment it sounds like a battle drum about to go to war.

I can hear Michael's and Daniel's thoughts in my head. They are going crazy, their emotions trying to consume everything inside me, but in this moment, the only thing I can focus on is Damon; his thoughts and emotions are the loudest and most dominant inside me, his soul wrapping around mine, holding it as tightly as he can.

"Damon, are you okay?" I whisper.

"You are asking me?"

"Yes, of course I am," I state, confused by his words. He slowly pulls me back from his chest. He releases his hold on me and wraps his arms tightly around me. His scent consuming me.

"I was going to ask you."

"Yes, I am okay."

"Are you sure? Your screams—" Damon stops and looks deeply into my eyes.

"I am sure," I whisper. He leans in and kisses me a quick kiss.

"We are impressed, Sky," the Angels state.

I take a deep breath and release my hold on Damon. I turn around and face them.

"You passed. You both passed…very impressive. You now know that this mate is true," they state, looking at Damon.

"I always knew he was true," I whisper, continuing to look at them.

"Can you say the same for your other two mates?" they ask me, looking at Michael and Daniel.

I take a deep breath and look at my other two mates. Both of them look from the Angels to me, their eyes filled with concern and worry, but not for them; the concern and worry is for me.

I look back at the Angels. "Yes, I can say the same for them."

"We will be the judge of that," they state, their tones making me a little nervous. If the other two trials are as painful as the first one was, I am a little worried.

"If you are true, there is nothing to worry about," one of the Angels states.

I look back at Damon; his breathing has finally slowed, his heartbeat not as rapid.

I look from Damon to Daniel and Michael, trying to figure out which one will be next, which one will have to go through the second trial with me. I slowly make my way between them and face the two Angels, their eyes watching me.

"Are you two ready for them?" I ask my mates.

"Yes," they both state, not needing any time to think about my question. All three of us look up at the Angels and wait for the next trial to start.

CHAPTER 60

Thunder Trial

Michael

I stand here next to Sky, looking up at the Angels, waiting for whatever is about to happen, and the only thing I can think about is her. She is the only one that has to go through all three trials. She is the only one that has to endure the pain the trials give three times. I shake my head and try to stay focused and prepared for whatever is about to happen, but I have a feeling that no matter how prepared we think we are, we will never be fully ready for what is about to take place.

I look at Sky and see that her breathing is becoming heavy. I can hear her thoughts and feel her emotions, and they are going wild. Her heart is beating so fast. I calmly reach over and grab her hand. She holds on tightly.

I look up at the Angels, and we all wait for whatever is in store for us. At first nothing happens. I can tell that Sky is getting more and more worried with each passing minute. It is so silent; the forest is not even making sounds. I think that it, too, is waiting for the next trial to start.

Sky and I both take a deep breath, and right when we do, clouds start to form over our heads. Sky and I both look up. The clouds are dark. I slowly look at Sky, and she looks at me. The clouds start to move around and start to lower.

I take another deep breath, and that is when the clouds let loose the loudest thunder sound I have ever heard. I look back up at the sky and see a lightning bolt coming straight down at Sky. I immediately release my hold on her hand and grab her arm and pull her into my arms. I hold her as tightly as I can. The lightning comes down and surrounds Sky and me, the thunder above making louder and louder screams through the sky. The wind begins to pick up as the lightning starts coursing through our bodies.

Sky shoves her head into my chest, trying not to scream.

Every passing second, the thunder gets louder and closer to us, the lightning not letting us go but instead consumes us completely. Sky lets out a scream. I can feel her tears through my shirt. It seems like the tighter we hold each other, the more angry the thunder and lightning becomes, sending down more bolts.

"Hold on, Sky!" I scream, the lightning hitting both of our hearts at the same time. I can feel our soul holding onto each other tightly, trying to hold on through the pain. I can feel the lightning coursing through my entire body.

I can feel Sky's pain on top of my own, us both trying to hold onto each other, refusing to let go.

"Do you love her?" the Angels state.

"Yes! Please…please stop hurting her!" I scream.

"What would you do for her?" they ask.

"Anything…anything!" I scream again, the lightning coming down more, the bolt more intense each time.

"What is your intention?"

"To love her…to protect her."

"Do you love him?" they ask Sky. She gently pulls her face from my chest and looks me in the eyes, tears still falling down her face.

"Yes, I love him," Sky whispers.

"What would you do for him?"

"Anything…just please stop…stop hurting him…please!" Sky screams.

"What is your intention?"

"To do the right thing!" Sky screams again. Another lightning bolt comes down and hits us both.

We both scream.

"We believe you both," the Angels state. As soon as the words leave their mouths, the thunder stops; the lightning slowly starts to be pulled up, the sky calling it back home. As soon as the lightning leaves our bodies, we fall to our knees. Sky leans into me and rests her forehead on my chest.

"Sky," I whisper.

"Yeah?"

"Are you okay?"

"I...I...I think so...are you?" Sky whispers, pulling her head back from my chest.

I slowly begin getting up to stand on my feet. I help Sky; she falls against me, both of our legs a little weak.

Sky and I both turn to the Angels. "Now you know, Sky," the Angels state.

"Know what?" Sky asks.

"That this mate, you can always count on. During the trial, he showed courage and strength, and most importantly, he was more concerned about what was happening to you than what was happening to him," one of the Angel states.

"We believe you...we believe the both of you," one of the Angels states, looking carefully at each of us. We stand there hoping that they will say more, yet again, they remain quiet and just watch us. Sky takes a deep breath.

"Are you sure you are okay?" She looks over at me, her eyes telling me that she is not fine, her thoughts telling me that she is uncertain and a little afraid.

CHAPTER 61

I Don't Know If I Can Do This

I stand here looking at Michael, him patiently waiting for my true answer of if I am okay. I am not okay. I don't know if I can do this. I don't know if I can go through with the last trial. I take a deep breath and just stare at him. I can hear my other two mates coming over to my side, them not wanting to touch me just yet; the pain from the bolts have not completely faded yet.

I bring my hands up and place them gently onto Michael's chest. His breathing has slowed, his emotions and thoughts no longer out of control. He is worried about me, I can see it in his eyes. All of my mates want me to say something—say anything—but in this moment, I can only remain silent, trying to process everything that just happened.

Nothing is at all what it appears to be. I never thought that this is what the trials would be or what they meant by being tested. The questions they have asked us has to do with me and my mates, not the dagger. I was on the wrong track, thinking that they would solely focus on our intentions with the dagger; they seem more worried about our intentions with each other.

I slowly drop my hands from Michael's chest. I look down and see that I am shaking—my hands are shaking, my knees are shaking; in fact, my whole body is shaking. Daniel steps forward and grabs both of my hands into his, his emotions filling my mind, my body, my soul. I look at his chest and watch his breathing; it is slow and steady.

"Sky, I need you to take a deep breath," Daniel whispers. I look up into his eyes. They are searching my face, his eyes pleading with me to do as he says.

I take a deep breath and slowly release it. "Again," Daniel states.

I take another deep breath and slowly release it. I watch him breathe with me.

"There you go, Sky, just keep breathing…okay…just keep breathing with me," Daniel whispers.

I do as he asks, focusing on my and his breathing.

"One last trial, Protector," the Angels state. I close my eyes and take another deep breath. When I open them, everyone is looking at me, my mates filled with worry and concern.

"I don't know if I can do this," I whisper.

"Yes, you can," Gabriel states.

I shake my head. "It's too painful, I don't know if I can."

"You're the strongest person we know. You can do this…we are almost done," Daniel states.

I shake my head. "I am not as strong as you all think I am."

"Sky, you are stronger than you realize. They need you—the world needs you," I hear one of the Angels state.

"The Angel is right, Sky, we need you," Michael states.

I take another deep breath. "Okay," is the only word I can say. I open my eyes and look at Daniel. He nods, letting me know that he is ready for the trial. That makes one of us. I don't know how much more pain I can take before I break.

But I can't stop now. We have come way too far for us not to finish, so I turn around and face the Angel, with Daniel and wait for the trial to begin.

CHAPTER 62

Ice Trial

Daniel

Sky holds my hand as tightly as she can with the strength and energy she has left. I can see that the other two trials has weakened her; she is trying to be strong, but I can hear her doubting thoughts. I need to be the one to be strong for her this time. She is always strong for all of us all the time, doing her best to keep us and everything else together. It is time that I step up and be that for her, in this moment.

We both take a step toward the Angels, them both looking down at us. I have no idea what is going to happen, but as long as I have Sky by my side, I know that I can get through this—we can get through this together.

I try and take a step closer to Sky, but I can't. I look down and see that my feet are covered in ice. I look over at Sky. Her eyes are wide; her feet are covered as well. I look up at the Angels. "Really?"

They say nothing but continue to watch us. I look down and see the ice beginning to come up both of our bodies. I hold on tighter onto Sky's hand. "Of course it had to be ice," I state to myself.

The ice slowly makes its way up our legs. I can feel the coldness from the ice entering into my bones.

"Do you love him?" the Angels ask Sky.

"Of course I do," she states, not needing any time to think. Hearing those words come out of her mouth soothes the pain the ice is causing. After everything I have done, she is still in love with me; she still loves me through everything.

"What would you do to save him?" one of the Angels ask Sky.

"What?" Sky replies, sounding confused by the question.

"What would you do to save him?" the Angel repeats the question.

"I would do anything—anything—to save him."

The ice continues up our legs and begins spreading across our stomachs; the pain starts to increase. I look over at Sky and can tell she feels it, too.

"Yes, I love her. I would do anything to save her. My intention is to protect her and be what she needs to me to be!" I scream, hoping my answers would make the pain stop, would make the ice stop from continuing to spread, but it doesn't.

The Angels look at me. "Thank you for your answers, but that is not what we were going to ask you."

My heart sinks. Of course they want to ask me different questions. Of course they are going to ask me something that I don't want to tell.

"Ask me...ask me anything, just please make it stop!" I scream.

The Angels are quiet for several moments, allowing the ice to continue to spread; my and Sky's hands are now frozen together.

"Ask me...ask me the questions!" I scream.

"What did the demon tell you about Sky?" the Angels state in a stern tone.

"What?" I ask.

Sky screams out as the ice begins to go up her neck.

"What did the demon tell you about Sky? About the dagger?" the Angels ask.

"Nothing," I state.

Sky screams again as the ice becomes more solid and begins going up her face.

"Okay...okay!" I scream.

"What did the demon tell you about Sky and the dagger?"

"He told me that she is the only one that can unleash its true power, that she is the only one that can wield it!" I scream.

"What would you do to save her?" the Angels ask.

I look over at Sky. Her mouth is almost covered in ice, her eyes allowing tears to fall.

"Anything… I would do anything to save her…to be with her…to love her."

"No more secrets," the Angels state.

"No more secrets," I state.

"We believe you, young Daniel," the Angels state.

The ice begins to melt away; the coldness in my bones is replaced with heat.

I take a deep breath. When the ice melts away from my feet, I fall to my knees. I look over at Sky. The ice melts away from her feet; she also falls to her knees. She looks at me, trying to catch her breath.

"No more lies," she states, looking at me dead in the eyes.

I look up at the Angels; their eyes have turned back to stone. Gabriel, Damon, and Michael stand in front of Sky and me. I can feel all of their anger burning through me.

"Your lies almost killed her," Gabriel states.

"I would have never let that happen," I reply, slowly standing up on my feet. I turn to help up Sky, but Damon is already helping her to her feet. She leans into him, allowing him to hold her weight.

"You almost did," Gabriel states.

I look into his eyes and see nothing but rage—rage that I have never seen before. He is finally showing how much he actually cares about Sky, something I thought he would never be able to do. Ever since he helped her with escaping the blue flame, I have seen something change in him; it has been burning slowly, but in this very moment, he is allowing it to come to the surface.

I take another deep breath and look at the entrance to Edanya; it looks the same. Nothing my eyes can see has changed.

"Now what?" I ask.

"You stay here…we will go put the dagger back together," Michael states.

"Seriously?" I state.

I watch them all nod. I look at Sky; she nods.

I watch Sky back away from Damon and gently take his hand in hers. She then turns to Michael and reaches for his hand. He is impatient and grabs her hand before she can grab his. Gabriel takes several steps toward the entrance and slightly turns around.

I watch him look at Sky, Damon, and Daniel, and then he turns back around and starts walking toward the entrance. I watch him stop right before entering; he takes a deep breath and walks over the threshold of the entrance.

The shield that I, at first, did not see shimmers as he walks through, different colors moving in all directions.

"Sky, be careful," I whisper.

She doesn't turn around but whisper, "You, too... I love you."

I watch my mate and Damon and Daniel begin taking steps toward the entrance. They walk through the threshold, the colors spreading again—the most beautiful colors. I stand here and wait, wait for them to return with the dagger, wait for her to return back to me.

CHAPTER 63

Entering the Waters of Edanya

Michael

We enter through the threshold. Sky holds my hand tightly. When we walk through the shield, everything is different: the sky is blue, no clouds in the sky, the birds fly over freely. I look around and see animals walking, playing, being with their own kind. They pay us no mind as we take more steps in the waters of Edanya. There are forests and waterfalls as far as the eye can see.

Sky releases my and Damon's hands and continues to take steps forward. "This place is magical," Sky states.

"Yes, it is," I state, walking to her side.

"Does it all look like this?"

"Yes...it is never-ending," I state, watching her scan the area.

I see her stop when she looks out into a forest; a mountain lies on the other side of it. "What is that?" She points.

"That is the forest of Edanya."

"What is the forest of Edanya?" she asks, looking from the forest to me.

"Maybe one day, I will tell you. For now just know it is known as the mountain of the future. Many go to that mountain to figure out their destiny," I state, looking at the mountain.

"I will keep you to that," Sky states.

"You know that I am man of my word," I state.

"Yes, Michael…yes, you are."

"Did you ever think that things would end this way when you started on this journey?" I ask, looking at her.

"No…but I didn't see a lot of things ending the way they have, but I can say that I am grateful for my mates and grateful for the things that have happened, even though some of the things were hard," Sky states, looking at me.

"You wouldn't do anything differently?"

"No," she states, not even needing to think more about my question.

"Why?"

"Because it has led me here, to you, to Damon, and to Daniel. I still don't know what will happen in the future, but I do know that I am lucky," she states, leaning in and kissing my cheek.

Her words catch me off guard. No matter what Barbas or anyone else tries to do to her, she always sees the good and does her best to do the right thing. I will never understand why the soul-bond chose me to be by her side, but I know that she is not the only one that is grateful for how things have turned out.

Sky pulls away and starts walking deeper into the waters of Edanya, looking at everything. I take a deep breath and follow her lead. It has been a long time since I have been here, and it still takes my breath away. She still takes my breath away.

CHAPTER 64

Piece of Paradise

Damon

This place is like nothing I have ever seen before. I was the prince of darkness for so long, living in hell, commanding my demons to kill and take over Mother Earth. I never thought that I would end up here in this beautiful place.

I look over at Sky. She is bent down, touching the green grass. Nothing has been touched by darkness in this place; it is protected, protected from creatures that I once was. I slowly make my way over to Sky. She is looking around, watching all the animals.

"They don't even mind that we are here," she states.

"Why would they? Nothing has ever harmed them. They have no reason to mind," I state, looking over at the deer eating grass.

Sky looks at me. Her eyes are filled with joy and amazement. "After everything that has happened, we have finally made it here."

"Yes, we have… I knew we would," I state, continuing to look into her eyes.

"Oh really?"

"Yes," I state.

"And why is that?" Sky asks, taking a step closer to me.

"Because, Sky, you don't know how to fail. You never let anything get in your way. You're the most motivated, determined person I know," I state, closing the rest of the distances between us.

She watches me, listening to my words, her eyes filled with passion and love.

"We need to find the stream," Gabriel states, walking over to us.

"Do you know where it is?" I ask, looking at him.

He nods. "Yes, I know where it is."

I watch Michael walk up behind Sky, all of them looking at me. I take a deep breath. Gabriel takes the three pieces of the dagger out of his pocket and holds them in his hands. I watch Sky walk over to Gabriel, and she calmly grabs the pieces from his hands.

I watch him watch her. I don't know how she does it, but she brings out the best in all of us and makes us all want to change for the better. Gabriel used to be so hard and distant, and now he has changed. The only person he shows any affection toward is Sky.

Gabriel turns around and starts walking toward a wooded area. All of us follow him, not saying anything, just watching and observing. I gently grab Sky's hand as we walk; she gladly takes it and squeezes my hand. This place is so big, as far as the eye can see. We would have never found this place if it wasn't for Michael and Gabriel.

If Eden looks anything like this or feels like this at all, I can see why the Angels guard it the way they do. I now understand a little better for the need of the trials.

CHAPTER 65

It All Comes Down to This Moment

I can hear Daniel's thoughts in my head; he is not excited nor happy about having to stay back. I do my best to reassure him that we won't be long, but my words do not help his anxiety and worry about not being with me.

I hold tightly onto Damon's hand, knowing very well that soon we will see the stream, the stream that will be able to put together the dagger. We then will be one step closer to stopping Barbas and putting an end to his rule.

I can feel my heart starting to beat faster with each step we take. Gabriel is taking us into a small wooded area surrounded by the most beautiful trees I have ever seen. They are not just strong; they are magical. I can feel their energy radiating off of them. Mother Earth is strong in this place and very powerful.

"Where is this stream at?" Damon asks, squeezing my hand.

"It is not far. It is right up ahead in that wooded area," Gabriel states, pointing ahead.

"So what will I have to do with the pieces again?"

"You place the pieces in the stream. You hold them together and let the water do the rest. It will only take it a few moments to put the dagger back together," Gabriel states.

"Will it hurt?"

I watch him stop and lightly turn and look at me. I watch him shake his head. "Nothing in Edanya will harm you, Sky. No, it will not hurt."

He turns back around and continues walking toward the small wooded area.

I look to each of my sides—Damon is on one side, and Michael is on the other; both of them are watching Gabriel. I look ahead and see that we are almost to the wooded area.

A few minutes pass, and we are finally about to enter the wooded area. I stop and take a good look at the tall strong trees. Birds are flying overhead. I look between the trees and see all kinds of animals playing, eating, not a care in the world, going about their business in their home that has been untouched by darkness.

Gabriel slightly turns around and whispers, "It is time, Sky, time to put the dagger back together."

I nod and take the first step into the wooded area and then begin taking more and more steps. Damon's hand is holding onto mine tightly. Michael is calmly walking beside me. He is calm; his heart is beating steady.

I see up ahead a small waterfall and a stream leading deeper into the forest. Gabriel picks up his pace, and we follow his lead, making our way over to the stream.

I take a deep breath when I take my last step that lands me directly in front of the stream. I release Damon's hand and fall to my knees. I look down and see the three pieces in one of my hands. I cautiously and gently start lowering my hand down to the stream. The water is clear; the rocks beneath the water are all different colors—blues, greens, yellows, reds, purples. I gently place the dagger into the stream, allowing the water to wash over my hand. I rest the back of my hand on the rocks and wait.

Damon and Michael both take their positions next to me, both kneeling down on one knee to watch what happens.

Gabriel is watching as well but from a distance. His breathing is calm. I can hear his heartbeat, like a calmly drum.

I take a deep breath and continue to look down at the dagger pieces in my hand under the water. After a few minutes, I go to turn to Gabriel, but then I see the blade being taken from my hand from the water; the water allows the dagger to sink down and lie on the colorful rocks. I lift my hand out of the water and watch; we all watch.

The water slowly starts bringing the three pieces together. I watch as the broken parts are put back together. What once was broken is now put back in its rightful place, as if the events done to it never happened. Gabriel was right—it only takes a few moment and the dagger lying on the rocks at the bottom of the stream has been made new.

I take a deep breath and put my hands into the water and gently take the dagger into my hands. I lift it out of the water and calmly begin to stand; my mates stand with me, both of them looking at the dagger and then looking at me.

"It is finished," I hear Gabriel whisper. I turn around and face him, holding the dagger in my hands.

I look down and look at the dagger. It looks different than I remember. The dagger is lighter; the color has changed. The only thing that remains the same are the markings going down the blade.

As I stand here and stare at it, the blade begins to glow blue, white, and black. I look up at Gabriel, and he is smiling.

"Daniel was right. You are the one that can unlock the power of the dagger."

I look back down at the dagger and watch the bright glow start to fade.

"What now?" I whisper.

"We go home," Damon states, taking a step closer to me.

I look to Gabriel; he nods.

I take a deep breath and wrap my fingers around the dagger. I nod. "We go home."

CHAPTER 66

Time to Go Home

Daniel

I can hear from Sky that the dagger has been put back together, and they are making their way back to me. My heart sinks, knowing that we are about to face Barbas once again. The last time we faced him in open battle, we lost and I got taken. And after that, everything changed; nothing will be like it was before.

I take a deep breath, pacing back and forth, back and forth, waiting for the moment that I get to see her again.

Bring it to me, Daniel, I hear in my mind. I stop and know right away that it is Barbas. Even though I passed the trial and told the truth, he still lives inside my head; he still lives inside of me.

"No!" I scream.

Bring me the dagger, Daniel, Barbas states calmly in my mind.

"I will not do what you ask."

"Oh, my son, you will," Barbas whispers.

I shake my head and resume my pacing. Every minute that goes by, Sky's thoughts get louder and louder. I know she is coming.

I stop at the entrance and wait, wait to see her face. After several minutes, I finally see Sky, Damon, Michael, and Gabriel walking toward the entrance. I look down at her hands; she is holding tightly onto the dagger.

I watch Sky stop at the threshold and look at me. Her eyes are filled with joy, happiness, but still a little concern.

I take a step forward. I watch as Damon, Michael, and Gabriel walk through the entrance. Sky stops and looks at me. A small smile forms on her lips, and she walks through the threshold. As soon as she does, I walk toward her, quickly wanting to have her in my arms.

I quickly close the distance between us and wrap my arms around her. She continues to hold onto the dagger tightly in her hands. After a few moments, I release my hold on her and take a step back.

"Sorry it took so long," Sky states. "But we did it, Daniel, the dagger is back the way it was, the way it was always meant to be."

"I see," I state, watching her.

"Are you ready to go home, Daniel?" Sky asks.

"Home?"

"The cottage. It is time that we go back home," Sky states. She leans forward and kisses my lips, sweet but quick. I want to lean in and make it deeper, but she backs away before I can.

"All of this for that thing right there?" I state, looking down at the dagger in her hands.

She nods.

I take a step forward and place my hands on top of hers. "Let's go home, Sky."

She smiles. We both look down at the dagger. I move my hands and slowly reach for the dagger. She opens her fingers, willingly giving it to me, allowing me to hold the dagger. I look into her eyes before taking it; her eyes are full of trust and love for me, her thoughts and emotions calm and steady.

I take the dagger from her hands and hold it in my own. The dagger is lighter than it was before; it looks different and feels different. Nothing happens when I take the dagger in my hands—no power comes forth, no beams of light, nothing; the blade it silent.

I hold the dagger in one hand and grab Sky's in the other.

Gabriel, Damon, and Daniel step forth, us all standing side by side.

I take a deep breath and release my wings from my back. Sky, Damon, and Michael do the same. I look over at Gabriel; he closes his eyes and calls the blue beam down.

It doesn't take long to surround him and lift him up off of the ground. I watch the blue beam take him up into the sky; we all watch as he disappears, and soon after, we all take off, heading to the place we call home, heading right toward Barbas.

CHAPTER 67

I Will Never Give In

Skyler

The demon has been silent, just watching me. Mother Earth has still not let up her pouring of the rain, the storm getting worse with every passing moment. I pace back and forth in front of the demon, waiting for Gabriel and the others to return. So far it has been quiet here. I am surprised that Barbas and the demons haven't tried anything.

"You preparing for what is about to happen?" the demon asks.

I stop and look at him; his eyes are dark, no soul can be found inside of him. "I am preparing for whatever comes, yes."

"No matter how much you prepare...whatever Barbas has planned, you will never be ready for it."

"So you say."

"Yes, I do. You have never fought against a prince like him. He is not like the others, far from it, in fact."

"I am not in the mood for your games, demon," I state, looking at the wooden door.

"But games are so much fun."

"Not your games," I state, trying not to feed into whatever head games he is trying to play.

I can feel his eyes on me. I look up at the sky and see how dark it has become, the storm not willing to let up, Mother Earth showing her rage, trying to be heard.

I take a deep breath and begin walking toward the wooden door.

"You know, eventually all of you will give in. You will give in."

I don't turn around. I place my hand on the doorknob and calmly state, "I will never give in."

I turn the doorknob and open the door, looking out at the dark field. It is still empty.

CHAPTER 68

The Dark Will Overtake the Light

Argo

I watch Skyler look out into the field, doing his best to keep watch. He must not be able to feel the demons and the prince that are close and watching, but I can. Not even the blue flames can keep me from knowing that they are close.

"They are coming for you. They are coming for all of you," I state.

He turns around and looks at me, not leaving the doorway.

"You have no idea what is coming, but soon, my friend, soon you will, and nothing can stop it," I state.

"You don't know everything, demon."

"No, I don't, but I do know this—everything you are fighting so hard for, everything that you have learned to love, that you are trying so hard to protect, all of it will be for nothing," I whisper.

Skyler looks at me, trying to hide his fear, but even through the blue flames, I can smell it. I can smell that he doesn't want to be here; he doesn't want any of this, but still he stays and follows out orders that, in the end, will get him killed.

"You have a choice, my friend. You can still choose to fight for the winning side."

"You are crazy," he states, looking from me back out to the field.

"Maybe…but don't say I didn't warn you or give you a way out. You will die. All of them will die," I state, allowing for a laugh to escape my lips.

"Talk all you want, demon, but right now, you are still locked up in the blue flame, and I am the one that is free."

"Maybe so, but the dark will overtake the light. Mother Earth will give into the prince, and nothing else will matter—none of this matters. Your side will lose," I state, feeling the blue-flamed chains going in deeper into my flesh.

I watch Skyler look out at the fields. He is trying to keep his breathing and heartbeat under control, but he can't; he is slowly losing control, my words entering into his mind, consuming every single thought he has.

So far, the only one winning at this game is me.

CHAPTER 69

You Know Nothing

Barbas

"It is time," I say to my men.

Sayble stands next to me. We begin making our way down the hill, toward the cottage. The fallen has opened the wooden door. I know Argo can feel us coming. I know that he knows that we are near. As we make our way down the hill, the storm above becomes more violent.

Nature is trying to warn them, warn all of them, but no one is listening. We make it down the hill and get to the back of the small wooden shed. I can hear Argo and the fallen breathing, both of them waiting to see what happens—if anything happens.

I slightly turn and look behind me and see all of my men—thousands upon thousands of demons and fallen we have transformed—all of them willing to follow me, do anything that I ask; they do it without question. I make it around the small wooden shed and slowly make my way to the wooden door.

I take the last few steps and turn and look at the fallen, the one they have ordered to watch over my demon. His eyes go wide. He doesn't move nor does he say anything. He looks behind me and sees my demons, my soldiers that have come. I can hear his heartbeat; it is very rapid and unsteady. I look past the fallen and see Argo in the blue flames; his eyes are deadlocked on me.

I look back at the fallen and take another step forward. He takes several steps back. I walk through the threshold of the door and step onto the yard. Mother Earth shakes when I enter, but she is unable to cast me out, the spell not able to keep me out.

"So you have been watching my demon?" I ask, looking straight into the fallen's eyes.

He doesn't say anything but instead takes another step back. I take several steps forward. I can hear my men starting to enter through the door, starting to surround the yard. I quickly close the distance between me and the fallen. He tries to step back, but I am too quick for him; my hand is already around his neck, keeping him in place. He struggles, trying to get free, but he can't.

"You can always turn him," I hear Argo state.

"I could…but that would be boring." As I say the words, I bring up my sword and run it through his heart. His eyes go wide and then slowly start to fade. I throw him down to the ground. I turn and look at Argo.

"They will be here soon," I state.

I turn and look at the wooden door and see Daniel standing there, the dagger in his hand. I knew that he would listen. I knew he was one of us. I take a small step forward and stop, waiting for him to enter the yard, but he doesn't; he stands still, watching me, searching my face.

I see behind him the Angel blue beam down to the ground, then Sky, Damon, and Michael slowly get lowered to the ground, all of them looking at me. I watch as they order their wings to lower down and enter back into their backs.

"Welcome home," I state, looking directly at Sky.

CHAPTER 70

I'm Sorry This Is How It Has to Be

Daniel

I stand in the doorway with the dagger in my hand. Barbas is smiling, knowing that we would come and knowing that I would find a way to get the dagger.

I take a step forward through the threshold of the doorway. I look around and see all the demons and the fallen that have given in to Barbas and his plan of them changing. They did not fight against the darkness; they willingly gave in to what Barbas was asking of them.

Many of the faces I see are of the demons that tortured me, that burned me, that were mocking me, that told me to give in to the darkness, but now I can't completely judge them for their behaviors, for I, too, have given in to the darkness. I to have submitted down to Barbas.

I take another step forward. I hear Gabriel, Sky, Damon, and Michael follow my lead. Soon I take enough steps where I am only a foot away from Barbas, and the others are now through the threshold of the wooden door. I hear Sky's thoughts, screaming at me to not move, screaming at me to give her the dagger, but I don't reply. I don't listen to her, for this is my fight—me and him. He wanted me to transform; he wanted me to give in to his desires, and now that I have, he will wish that I never did.

Sky doesn't understand my silence. I hear her take another step forward. She places one of her hands on my back. "Daniel," she whispers.

I don't respond; my eyes are still deadlocked onto Barbas. "Daniel, please give me the dagger…please."

"I can't," I finally whisper.

"What? Why? Daniel—"

"Sky, I love you…just know that, okay? I'm sorry, but this is how it has to be."

"Daniel, please. I am begging you."

I shake my head and continue looking at Barbas. The demons surrounding us take a step forward, all of them prepared to die for their prince.

CHAPTER 71

Taken by Fire

I lower my hand from Daniel's back and take a step back. Damon is standing behind me; my back leans against his chest. He places his hands on my shoulders. I take a deep breath.

"Sky, welcome home. We have been waiting for you. I have been waiting for you," Barbas states, not hiding his amusement.

I stay where I am, partly because I don't want to get closer to him if I don't have to, and secondly because Damon's hands on my shoulders get tighter, and he is sending me warnings in my head to not even think about moving.

"So it all comes down to this?" I ask.

"Yes, I guess it does. You and I have been playing games, Sky, and it is time for the games to finally end."

"You are the one that has been playing games. You are the one that started all of this," I state, not hiding my anger.

A smile begins to form across his lips. "Yes, I guess I have…and now we all are here."

I watch Barbas look at Argo in the blue flames, and then he looks directly past me, to Gabriel. "Do you think you can let my demon go now?"

"You're kidding, right?" I ask.

I watch him shake his head. "Actually no, I am not kidding. I am actually very serious."

"Your demon is where he is meant to be," Damon states from behind me.

"That is funny coming from you, the one who turned on his own kind," Barbas states as his hands form into fists.

"We all have choices, Barbas. I have made mine," Damon states.

Barbas shakes his head and continues to look at me. "You have changed since the last time I held you in my arms."

"A lot has changed since then," I state.

"Enough…enough with the games, Barbas!" Daniel yells.

I watch Barbas turn his eyes from me to Daniel. "You know, I didn't think you would be able to do it, but here you are, with the dagger in your hand. Now give it to me."

"Daniel, what he is talking about?" I ask in a concerned voice.

"Oh, he never told you? Me and him have been talking. I told him to bring me the dagger, and I knew you would allow him to hold onto it," Barbas states.

"Daniel…what he is talking about?"

"He asked me to bring him the dagger," Daniel whispers, not turning around to look at me.

"No…no you wouldn't…Daniel, you can't give him that dagger, not after everything we have been through, please…please don't do this!" I scream.

"Sky, now, now, begging does not suit you very well," Barbas states, reaching out his hand to Daniel. "Give me the dagger," he states.

I feel Damon release my shoulders, and gently his arms wrap around my stomach; he holds on tightly…preparing to keep me in place.

I watch Daniel take a small step toward Barbas. I take a deep breath. *He wouldn't*, I tell myself, *he wouldn't betray me.*

Daniel looks down at Barbas's hand and then looks at the dagger in his hand. Slowly he starts bringing the dagger closer and closer to Barbas's hand. Right when I am about to scream at him to stop, Daniel quickly takes the blade and cuts across Barbas's hand.

Barbas looks at Daniel and then looks at me; his eyes are wide. I see the dagger pulling in the shadows coming from his wound.

Daniel turns around slightly to look at me, and he mouths *I love you*. He turns back around and stabs Barbas's right, where his heart used to be.

All the demons around us start screaming, flames coming up from the ground, starting to work its way up their bodies. Barbas falls to the ground. He looks at me, blood falling from his mouth, his eyes growing darker, the power leaving his body. Moments later, he falls to the ground by Daniel's feet. I watch Daniel take a deep breath, and then he turns around.

I want to run to him, but Damon's grip around my stomach gets tighter, making sure I can't move even if I tried. Daniel looks at me; his eyes are distant.

I watch Daniel start to lift the dagger. He points the dagger at his heart.

"Daniel, what are you doing?" I scream.

I watch him take a deep breath. "I love you, Sky, please always remember that."

I watch as he brings the dagger closer and closer to his heart.

He stops right before it enters, looking at all of us. I watch as a single black tear escapes from his eyes, falling down his face. When the tear hits the ground, my lover, my mate, pushes the dagger into his heart. Black flames come up from the ground, quickly consuming him.

"No!" I scream. I begin falling to my knees. Damon falls down with me, his grip getting tighter. Thousands of blue, black, and white tears fall from my eyes.

And just like that, my lover—my mate—was gone, and so were his demons. The only thing that remains is the dagger lying on the ground.

To be continued…
Stay tuned for book 4, *Unveiled: Consumed by Fire*

About the Author

Sasha R.C. is the author of the *Unveiled* series. She overcame her addiction to alcohol and drugs and now lives a life of recovery. All thanks to her higher power and her strong support system of family and friends. She now reaches out to help others overcome that same addiction as an alcohol and drug counselor.

Sasha loves getting lost in a good book—anything fantasy or romance that includes vampires, werewolves, magic, dragons, demons, and angels.

Sasha currently resides in Oregon, with her husband and two dogs, Smokey and Bandit. Sasha is currently writing the last two books in the *Unveiled* series.

CPSIA information can be obtained
at www.ICGtesting.com
Printed in the USA
BVHW031928130423
662314BV00001B/2